AUTUMN SPICE ON SUNFLOWER STREET

A DELIGHTFULLY COSY AND UPLIFTING READ

SUNFLOWER STREET
BOOK 3

RACHEL GRIFFITHS

COSY COTTAGE BOOKS

Created with Vellum

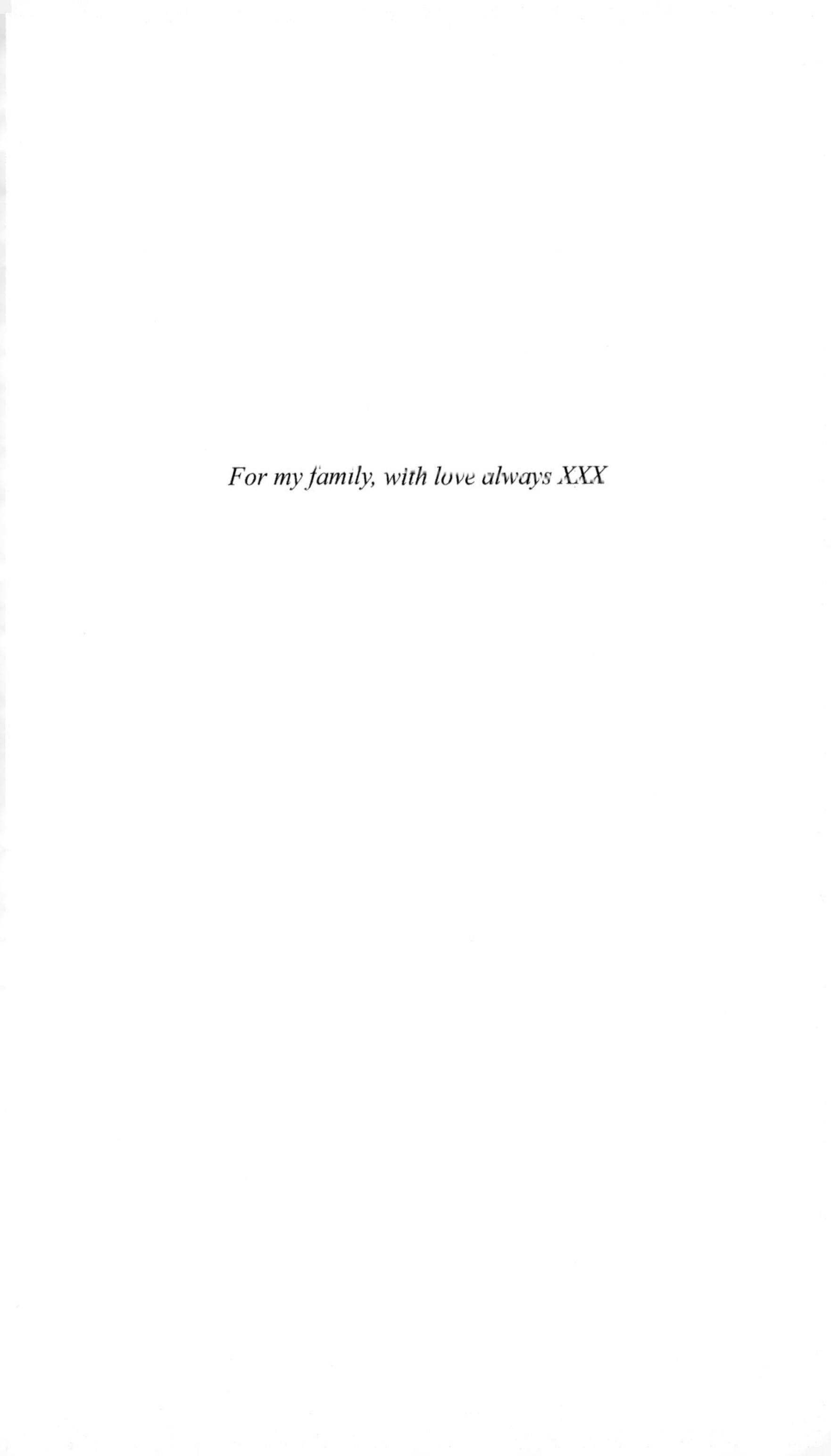

For my family, with love always XXX

AUTUMN SPICE ON SUNFLOWER STREET

Joanne Baker often feels like she's drifting through life. She's thirty-two, works at the local café and still lives with her parents. She tells people it's because she's saving for a mortgage deposit, but the real reason she hasn't moved out is something she doesn't want to admit to anyone…

Until she faces up to the maxed-out credit cards, never worn clothes and impractical shoes still in their boxes, she can't even begin to think about saving. She needs help, and when her friends Roxie and Lila find out the truth, they offer their support.

As autumn arrives on Sunflower Street, bringing cold crisp days and cosy nights, Joanne feels the pressure of Christmas on the horizon. She needs to sort her life out before another year passes by. It doesn't help that her perfect older sister has her life completely together with her perfect career, perfect husband and perfect children.

Making changes can be difficult, but it's not impossible, and when Joanne puts her trust in those around her, she learns that the perfect life is an illusion, and that everyone has their own struggles along the way.

Taking the first step in the right direction is daunting, but having loving friends and family in her corner, means that Joanne has the opportunity to make a fresh start.

1

Joanne Baker's mobile phone pinged with an incoming message and she glanced at it where it lay on the kitchen table, screen down. Her mum and dad looked up expectantly, her mum from her crossword and her dad from his iPad. Joanne forced herself to reach for her mobile and turn it over. She saw that the text was from the bank, so she set the phone back down.

'Not going to reply?' her mum asked, peering over the top of her glasses.

'It can wait.' Joanne picked up the muffin she'd been enjoying and stuffed the rest of it in her mouth, no longer able to taste the vanilla and blueberry flavours, because the text message had been an all too familiar reminder about her expanding overdraft. She washed the muffin down with coffee then ran a thumb around the small plate to catch the crumbs. No sense wasting food, she thought, even if she wasn't enjoying it.

She got up and put the kettle on, needing another coffee before she went upstairs to get ready for her shift at the café. While she waited for it to boil, she gazed out of the kitchen window at the back garden. Her parents' house on Sunflower Street was small but well-maintained. Her dad was a keen gardener, keeping the lawn in good order, feeding it regularly and pulling out any weeds that dared to sprout in the perfect rectangle of green. Bordering the grass were flower beds where roses, hydrangeas, lilies, tulips and more flowered during the warmer months, but now, with it being early October, her dad had pruned the rose bushes back and the summer flowers were gone.

At the bottom of the garden, there was a greenhouse to the left and to the right was a large shed. Her parents grew a variety of vegetables in the greenhouse in the summer and her dad used the shed as a retreat throughout the year, locking himself in there whenever he wanted some peace and quiet, or at least he had until Joanne started using it for storage.

Joanne made three coffees then set two of them on the table in front of her parents.

'Thanks, Joanne.' Her mum smiled.

'Thanks, love.' Her dad nodded.

'You're welcome. I'm going to get ready for work.' Joanne grabbed her mobile and her coffee then made her way upstairs.

She closed the bedroom door behind her, put her coffee on the bedside table then sat on her bed and swiped her phone screen. The text from the bank was nothing alarming, just informing her that she had a new message in her internet banking folder, but she knew it wouldn't be good news and her stomach churned in the way it had a habit of doing now. It was only the start of the month and pay day was weeks away, plus Joanne's pay wasn't going to go far at all. It never did anymore.

How she'd got herself into such a mess so quickly, she didn't know, but she had no idea how to get herself out of it. Most of the time she just ignored it, hoping it would go away, be like one of those stories where it had all been a dream.

If only that were true . . .

Three hours later, Joanne was at work, the café bustling with the lunchtime rush of local pensioners socialising, mums and dads with toddlers on play dates, and people popping in from local businesses to grab takeaway sandwiches. She was already sweaty as she tried to keep up with the constant stream of orders and her feet ached in her worn trainers. She had other pairs at home that she could wear, but she didn't like to in case her colleagues thought she was being paid more than them or in case the café owner, Bridget Wibberley, thought she wasn't in need of the pay rise she'd requested at her six monthly review. In all fairness, Bridget was a good boss, kind and understanding, but even the rise she had agreed to hadn't really helped Joanne. Things had become far too messy for that.

'Penny for them!'

The familiar voice cut through Joanne's thoughts and she looked up to find her friend Roxie Walker peering curiously at her. She took in Roxie's flushed cheeks, pink and yellow

Lycra outfit, and long black hair pulled into in a high ponytail with a wide headband that matched her Lycra.

'Hi, Roxie. Have you been working out?'

'I went for a run and I feel fabulous, darling. I thought I'd grab a coffee before heading home to shower.'

'Skinny latte?' Joanne asked.

'Please.' Roxie pulled a bank card from her purse and held it to the reader. 'Are you all right today?'

Joanne nodded as she made the coffee, taking care to use skimmed milk because Roxie would have a fit if she ended up with full-fat. 'I'm fine. Just a bit tired, really. I didn't sleep that well last night.'

'Sorry to hear that.' Roxie frowned. 'You should come for a run with me. Exercise is wonderful for improving sleep quality.'

Joanne laughed, but inside she found herself wishing she had half Roxie's energy. Working long hours at the café where she was on her feet all day left her exhausted most evenings, and although she tried to get to yoga classes at the village hall on Saturday mornings, apart from that she didn't exercise at all. Unless you counted walking from the lounge to the kitchen to get the biscuit tin. She'd often thought that standing up all day should burn enough calories to make her slimmer. It worked for Bridget who, in her mid-forties, was more than ten years older than Joanne, but then she had a feeling that her boss wasn't constantly stuffing comfort food into her mouth. Not that Joanne was huge, she knew that, but she had gone up two sizes in the last year (depending on where she bought her clothes) and she was starting to worry that she'd keep getting bigger if she didn't do something about it soon. It wasn't even that she didn't like being curvy, because she did, and at five foot ten, she was tall enough to carry some extra weight, but with her mum being diabetic, Joanne knew that she had to be careful.

Joanne's mum had been diagnosed with type 2 diabetes in her fifties and she fought a constant battle to try to stay healthy. Joanne was at risk of developing the disease because it could be hereditary, and she knew that lifestyle could play a big part in it too. Every week began with her vowing to eat healthily and to do more exercise but by Wednesday her willpower tended to wane and by the time Friday came around, she was tucking back into cakes and biscuits again. The muffin she'd had this morning was one of her mum's healthy bakes, made with wholewheat flour, low-fat spread and sweetened with fruit juice, but even so, Joanne couldn't undo the family-sized bar of chocolate she'd eaten in bed the night before or the bacon and sausage roll she'd inhaled when she arrived at work.

'There you go, Roxie.' Joanne set the skinny latte on the counter. 'Glenda not with you?' She peered over the counter looking for the small pug.

'Not today. She's at home with Fletcher. We're still enjoying the novelty of having him around on Monday mornings.'

Joanne smiled. She knew how delighted Roxie had been when Fletcher had taken voluntary redundancy that summer. He'd always worked long hours in the City and Roxie had missed him, but then he'd decided that enough was enough and that he wanted to spend more time at home with his wife and dog. It was working out well for them.

'Well, have a great day!' Joanne nodded as Roxie blew her a kiss then sashayed out of the café, her small, pert bottom more like that of a teenager than a woman approaching fifty.

'One breakfast baguette and one cheese omelette.' Daniel Pugh, the café chef called from the hatch that opened up from the kitchen into the café.

'Coming!' Joanne picked up the plates then carried them over to the corner table where an elderly couple were waiting. She plastered on her best smile and decided to try to focus on her job and to forget about her worries until later, because nobody wanted their food served by a grumpy waitress. It wasn't good for business or fair on the customers, and the last thing Joanne wanted was to have people complaining about her.

She needed this job; without it, her finances would be even more of a concern.

2

Later that week, on Saturday morning, Joanne lay on her yoga mat in the village hall trying to concentrate on what Finlay Bridgewater was telling the class to do. The local yoga instructor and personal fitness trainer had a very calm and soothing voice and Joanne had often found herself falling asleep as he guided her through child's pose and then to shavasana.

Lying on her back in the cool hall that smelt of baking, old books and coffee, Joanne was at her most relaxed. Yoga tended to take her to the brink of consciousness where she teetered, craving the oblivion of sleep. It was, in fact, the only time she really felt herself relax these days and so she looked forward to the Saturday morning sessions that she usually attended with her friends Roxie and Lila. Most Saturdays, Joanne had to get to work afterwards, but as long as she made the early session, she didn't have to miss out.

'That's it everyone, focus on the start of each breath then slowly release it, feel your lungs completely empty before refilling them. Gooood . . . That's very, very gooood.'

Joanne's body sank even deeper into the mat and she started to drift, carried along on a small boat that bobbed on a lake. The sun shone down, warming her skin and the scent of coconuts and vanilla teased her nostrils. The masseur, who had appeared suddenly and from out of nowhere, pushed thumbs into the knots in Joanne's shoulders then stroked her hair back from her face.

'Joanne!'

She blinked. And again. Looked up into Roxie's smiling face.

'Oh. Hello.'

'You feel asleep, darling.'

'Again.' Lila said from her side.

'Oops.' Joanne accepted Roxie's hand and sat up. 'Was I snoring?'

Roxie nodded and Joanne winced.

'Ah well . . . ' Joanne looked around but no one was staring; they were all rolling up their mats and pulling on trainers, hoodies and jumpers. 'Everyone's used to me snoozing now.'

Roxie smiled. 'They certainly are.' Then she knitted her brows. 'Are you still not sleeping well?'

Joanne got to her feet then started to roll her mat but it went wonky, so she let it unroll then started again.

'Not the best. I think I need to stop eating chocolate before bed. Perhaps the caffeine and sugar are disagreeing with me.'

'It's possible.' Roxie nodded. 'Try some warm milk instead.'

'I will tonight.' Joanne slid the mat into its bag then pulled her trainers on.

'Do you have time for a coffee before work?' Roxie asked. 'Or shall we come to the café?'

'Yes I have time. I don't start until eleven and if I go there early, I'll probably end up helping out so I won't be able to chat.'

'Let's go back to mine then and grab a bite to eat.'

As they left the hall, they waved their thanks to Finlay who nodded his acknowledgement, then they walked out into the cold crisp October morning.

Half an hour later, Joanne was sitting at Roxie's kitchen table with a large mug of milky coffee and a plate of buttery toast in front of her. She was still in her Lycra so would need to pop home to change and shower before work but she had an hour to relax with her friends first. She was as comfortable sitting in silence with Roxie and Lila as she was when they chatted about anything and everything. Well . . . just about everything because there was one secret that Joanne hadn't shared with her friends and she didn't know how she ever would. It was her secret shame and she wasn't even sure they'd understand.

She glanced up from her toast now and then. Roxie looked incredibly chic today in her black yoga gear from one of those classy websites where even a yoga bra cost more than Joanne earned in a week. Her hair was swept back in a pony-tail and her lashes looked long and glossy like she'd painted them with oil. Then there was Lila, petite, blue-eyed and blonde haired with flawless pale skin. Next to them both, Joanne always felt clunky and tall, like the odd one out, but she knew that neither of them would see it that way. They were kind and compassionate women who constantly told one another why they were important, valued friends, and Joanne knew that they cared about her. It was her issue that she felt physically awkward, not theirs, and she couldn't imagine them saying a bad word about her; they had only ever treated her with respect and kindness.

Earlier in the year, Lila had gone through a very tough time after splitting with her fiancé and it had been Roxie and Joanne who had done their best to help her pull through. Along with the lovely Ethan Morris who had, at that point in time, recently returned to the village. He'd gone to Lila's to do some decorating and he and Lila had fallen in love. Joanne adored seeing them together because they made such a sweet couple and she loved seeing her dear friend so happy. Then there was Roxie and her husband, Fletcher, who'd been together for the majority of their lives. They were closer than ever after a blip in the summer and planned on renewing their wedding vows. Fletcher had proposed to his wife that summer, asking her to renew their vows so he could prove that he loved her as much as always.

As for Joanne, she had no special someone in her life. She didn't mind, most of the time, and had far too much to deal with anyway. Being in a relationship now would only complicate things further and that was the last thing she needed.

She shoved another piece of toast in her mouth, savouring the salty butter on her tongue and the fluffy texture of the thick toast. Food never let her down because she always knew exactly how it was going to make her feel.

'So ladies, I have news!' Roxie flashed them a dazzling smile.

'You've set a date?' Joanne asked hopefully.

'Oh . . . no, not yet. We're thinking that we might renew our vows after Christmas or in the new year.' Roxie raised her eyebrows. 'We want to plan it so it's really special. However, seeing as how it's October and just four weeks until Halloween, Fletcher and I thought we might host a party.'

'A Halloween party?' Lila asked.

'Yes!' Roxie rubbed her hands together. 'A proper affair with a marquee in the garden and decorations and lights, music and spooky food and so on. What do you think?'

'It would be lovely to have that to look forward to,' Lila said, her eyes lighting up.

'It's going to be fancy dress.' Roxie sipped her coffee.

'Does that mean we need to buy costumes?' Joanne's heart fluttered as she thought about searching for a suitable costume, about the glossy websites that would feature glamorous affairs in bright colours and about the numerous possibilities. She could be a witch, a vampire, a cat, a zombie. She could dress in something sophisticated or funny, perhaps come as a movie character. She could . . .

Her heart sank as she thought about how much a decent costume would cost. She could pick up a cheap one that might be made of nylon and fake velvet and fit her badly, possibly come undone at the seams, or she could look for something better, but that would cost more and right now, she needed to watch every penny.

'I could make something.' Lila put her toast down and dusted the crumbs off her hands. 'Does it have to be scary or can it be obscure?'

'Well, I was thinking horror themed, but you can be more random if you like.' Roxie shrugged. 'Up to you really. Have a think and see what you come up with.'

'I can't wait to tell, Ethan. He'll be as excited as me about this. We could create something together.'

'What about you, Joanne?' Roxie asked.

Joanne pouted. 'I could come as a . . . ghost.' Yes, that would avoid spending. She could grab one of her mum's old sheets and cut some holes in it and wear it over her head. That way, no one would see her embarrassment at not being more inventive.

'A ghost?' Roxie seemed to deflate in front of Joanne's eyes.

'Uh . . . yes. Perhaps.' Joanne coughed then took a swig of coffee to wash down the toast that was lodged in her throat. 'Or something else. I need to have a think about it.'

'Joanne . . . ' Roxie licked her lips. 'Is everything okay? I don't want you to think that Lila and I have been talking about you behind your back or anything, but we are both a bit concerned and have discussed those concerns. You're just quite tired all the time and you often seem distant, as if you've a great worry weighing you down. Is there something on your mind, darling? You can tell us and we'll help you, you know.'

'Absolutely.' Lila nodded. 'We'll always be here for you just as you've been here for us.'

Joanne lowered her gaze to her plate and swallowed hard. She loved her friends and knew they meant what they said but as heat crawled up her neck and into her cheeks, she also knew she couldn't share this with them. How could she when she couldn't even admit the full extent of her problem to herself?

Her mobile pinged and she turned it over on the table, cold dread seeping into her bones as she anticipated what the message would be about. As she scanned the text, her eyes widened, and her heart started to race.

'Oh god. Oh no . . . '

'What is it, honey?' Roxie reached for her free hand and held it between both of hers. 'You look like you've seen a bloody ghost.'

Joanne looked from Roxie to Lila and back again then she dropped her mobile phone as if it had burnt her hand.

'Can I look?' Roxie asked.

Joanne nodded. She couldn't manage to speak, couldn't get the words she wanted out, so instead she covered her face with her hands and started to cry. What did it matter if Roxie and Lila knew anyway? Things were so bad that she couldn't summon the energy to fight anymore. The thought of what her parents would think and say swept over her and made her cry harder. She had never wanted to disappoint them, only ever wanted to make them proud, but now she really was going to let them down and in spectacular style!

3

ou'll be here for lunch today, won't you?' Joanne's mum asked her as she handed her a mug of tea the next morning.

'Lunch?' Joanne frowned.

'Yes, you know, Sunday lunch. I've got a joint of beef and I'll make Yorkshire puds, roast potatoes and a trifle.'

'Yum.' Joanne nodded, although the prospect of a roast dinner didn't seem as appealing at 7.30 as it would at 1 p.m.

'So will you be here?'

'Of course.' Joanne sipped her tea. 'Where else would I be?'

'Wonderful,' her mum replied ignoring Joanne's question, 'because your sister is coming with Jeremy and the children.'

Joanne immediately regretted agreeing to be present. Now she couldn't invent an excuse and escape before her perfect sister with her perfect husband and perfect children arrived. Lunch would no doubt involve Kerry and Jeremy bragging about their jobs (assistant head teacher and senior accountant), their massive house, their highly accomplished children (Lottie aged five and Henry aged three) and their next holiday. They jetted off at least twice a year to places like the Maldives and Sicily, locations that sounded incredible but where Joanne would never be able to afford go. She wasn't even sure how they managed to afford the lifestyle they enjoyed because she didn't think teachers earned that much, and although Jeremy was a partner in the accountancy firm where he worked, from what Joanne could see, Kerry and Jeremy liked to spend money. A lot of money. Perhaps they'd received a large inheritance from his grandmother who'd died two years earlier or perhaps his parents, both retired professionals, gave them generous handouts.

Joanne preferred not to think about it too much because her sister was everything that she wasn't: successful, rich and perfect. Joanne couldn't understand how her parents wouldn't compare the two of them every single day. It would be inevitable that they did because their eldest daughter had done all that was expected of her and more, then there was Joanne who . . . well, had quite simply been a disappointment from day one. She had taken longer to walk, preferring to sit on her backside and watch as Kerry strutted her stuff. She had not done that well at school, preferring to leave her homework to the very last minute and often forgetting about it, then finding revision so tedious she often fell asleep while trying to revise and she had abandoned A levels after the first year and gone travelling. Kerry, on the other hand, had scored perfect grades, gone off to university, met Jeremy, got a teaching post then two more as she climbed the career ladder while also getting married and having two children.

Yes, Kerry was a success, a daughter any parents would be proud of, but Joanne was a let down, and things were getting worse all the time. Wait until she told her mum and dad what she'd confessed to Roxie and Lila yesterday. She sank onto a chair at the kitchen table and buried her face in her hands.

'It's not that bad is it, love?' Joanne's dad squeezed her shoulder then kissed her forehead.

'Morning, Dad.'

'I just told her that Kerry and the clan are coming for lunch,' Joanne's mum explained.

'Ahhh . . . ' Her dad sat next to her and poured a mug of tea. 'Be nice to see them, won't it?'

Joanne met his kind eyes over the teapot. How could she hurt him by disagreeing?

'Yes. Of course. I can't wait.'

'Good, good.' He patted her hand then sipped his tea. 'Great brew this, Hilda.'

'I do make a good brew, don't I?'

'You do.' He smiled. 'Hilda makes a good brew it's true.' He chuckled at the rhyme and Joanne's mum rolled her eyes affectionately.

'Right, I'm off to the shop for some fresh veg so you two keep an eye on the beef, won't you?'

'It's not in the oven already, is it?' Joanne's dad looked concerned; he was a man who liked his meat served medium rare.

'No, of course not, Rex. It's on the side though, out of the packaging, and Cindy Clawford must not be allowed to get her paws on it.'

'I'll keep my eyes peeled.' He nodded.

Joanne scanned the room for the old cat but she couldn't see her, so it was highly likely that she was upstairs on her parents' bed where she often slept. Joanne couldn't understand it herself, how her mum and dad could stand having the cat fur on their pillows and under the duvet, but they doted on the fluffy grey Persian and let her do whatever she liked. Joanne wasn't fussy on Cindy C though, as she'd been scratched many times for simply trying to get the cat to move off the sofa and the kitchen chairs, and sometimes, just for walking past her. Cindy Clawford had a notoriously bad temper and she seemed to take it all out on Joanne.

'Do you want to tell your old man what's wrong?' her dad asked her now that her mum was out of earshot.

'Nothing.' Joanne's voice wavered and she knew he wouldn't be convinced.

'I don't believe that, Joanne. Something's clearly bothering my girl and I'm here to help in any way I can.'

Joanne looked at him, this man who had always been there for her, with his shiny bald head, hazel eyes and thick moustache that always made her think of Tom Selleck. He had never been anything other than kind, always been a loving dad she could run to with her worries, although she tried not to cry in front of him because tears made him panic. But this worry that she'd been carrying around for the past two years was more than she wanted to lay at his slipper clad feet. It would shock him, concern him and she worried that he'd never look at her the same way again. Yes, she was no Kerry, but she knew she was loved and didn't want to cause her parents even more disappointment. Her biggest fear, though, was that they would try to help and that it would ruin them. They were both retired and didn't have much, didn't live a life of excess, but they would want to try to help financially and that thought broke her heart. She wanted to find a way to do this that didn't destroy their bank balance or ruin their retirement and turn it into one of constant money worries.

'I'm okay, Dad, honestly.' Joanne drained her mug then reached for the teapot.

'Is it because Kerry's coming?' he asked gently.

'It will be nice to see them all.' Joanne replied, swallowing her true feelings because they would upset him. He wanted his family to be united and to believe that Joanne and Kerry were close. It couldn't be further from the truth, sadly, but Joanne would let him have that because he deserved to be happy. He deserved to have peace of mind about that one thing at least, because if, or probably when Joanne did pluck up the courage to tell him about her money issues, she had a feeling that he was not going to sleep well for some time.

❧

When the doorbell went at 1 p.m., Joanne's heart sank to her socks. Knowing that there were several hours ahead where she'd have to listen to Kerry and Jeremy droning on about how well they were doing and how amazing their children were, was not something she could summon much enthusiasm for. However, even though her sister and brother-in-law could be boring and bordering on narcissistic, their children were delightful. Joanne loved spending time with Lottie and Henry and was often able to use them as an excuse to escape the adult conversation by taking them into the garden to play.

She gave her hair a quick brush and pulled it into a ponytail then left her bedroom and crossed the landing. Jeremy's monotone voice drifted up the stairs as he complained about the traffic on the journey there, about how most drivers didn't have a clue about the Highway Code and how incredibly small the village seemed. Joanne sucked in a deep breath and forced her mouth into a smile. The best way to deal with Jeremy was to show no emotion because he was one of those people who liked to try to rile others, especially, for some reason, his sister-in-law. In the past, Joanne had retaliated, but experience had taught her that there was no point because Jeremy was like some sort of emotional vampire that fed off the distress of others. Perhaps it was because he worked with numbers all day so he lacked people skills or perhaps it was because he had an entitled air about him that had been generated by having everything he ever wanted without too much of a struggle – Joanne's sister included.

She exhaled and gave herself a shake. This kind of thinking wasn't doing her or anyone else any good and she needed to stop. Jeremy wasn't a bad man; he was just a bit of a knob sometimes, but wasn't that true of most people? He could probably say the same about Joanne.

Descending the stairs, Joanne saw Kerry in the hallway: ginger hair in its smooth bob, silky white blouse crease free, fawn slacks and brown leather pumps smart casual for Sunday lunch. There were pearls in her ears and round her neck and she looked like Joanne had always thought a head teacher should look. Kerry wasn't a head teacher yet, but she was on the way to becoming one, and she would, no doubt, have achieved that position by the time she reached her mid-forties. Kerry had always been ambitious and when she set her sights on something, she went for it single-mindedly. Joanne often wished she had half her sister's drive, but then if that meant marrying someone like Jeremy who completed the whole (apparently) perfect package, she didn't know if she could be like her.

Jeremy was behind Kerry: his thinning blond hair exposed from above, his wiry frame evident in his navy polo shirt and cream chinos, his skin so pale it was almost translucent. As she reached the bottom stair and Jeremy's gaze landed on her, she could see the blue vein that ran across his temple, a vein that bulged and pulsed when Jeremy became animated. She realised that she was still smiling and tried to adjust her expression so her face wasn't frozen like that of a demented clown, but her lips merely twitched; clearly her body wasn't going to play ball today. When Lottie came running from the kitchen, Joanne was relieved that she could look away and give her attention to the beautiful child instead.

'Aunty Jo!' Lottie flung herself at Joanne and she scooped the little girl up, warmth flooding through her as Lottie wrapped her arms around her neck.

'Lottie Loo!' Joanne giggled as Lottie blew raspberries on her cheeks, something the little girl had done to Joanne since she was a baby. 'Stop it! That tickles.'

'Say you surrender!' Lottie leant back and met Joanne's gaze then resumed raspberry blowing.

'I surrender.'

'Lottie cut that out. Your aunt does not want your slobbery kisses all over her.' Jeremy's nasal tones clipped through the air and Joanne felt the warmth of her laughter seeping away.

She gently lowered Lottie to the floor, trying to stay calm and not to bite. This was typical Jeremy and it would do no good to tell him that a five-year-old child should be able to have a bit of fun with her aunt. He'd have some answer prepared to fire at her and Joanne would end up getting annoyed then upset and she didn't want that, not today.

'Hello, Joanne.' Kerry smiled then gave her a quick kiss on the cheek. 'You're looking well.'

'Thanks. You too.'

Joanne felt Jeremy's eyes upon them and knew he'd be comparing his wife with his sister-in-law, probably glad he hadn't married the younger one. In stretchy jeans with a baggy black T-shirt, Joanne knew that she looked far more casually attired than Kerry and far more curvaceous. But then Kerry was constantly on the go and she'd confessed in the past that she often skipped lunch if she had meetings or pupils in detention. She lived, she had said, on coffee and adrenaline, which didn't sound particularly healthy to Joanne.

'Let's go and see Nanny.' Lottie tugged on Joanne's hand and she let the small girl lead her to the kitchen, watching Lottie's blonde curls bounce as she walked. She resembled her dad more than her mum but she was a beautiful child and Joanne hoped she'd grow up to be nothing like her dad at all. But who knew what someone would be like as an adult? There could have been a time when Jeremy was a sweet, playful child but Joanne found it hard to imagine him ever being anything other than uptight, snobby and boastful.

In the kitchen, Joanne's parents were cooing over tiny Henry as he showed them a scab on his knee and relayed the story of how it happened in his sweet high voice complete with an adorable lisp. He was a shy child and followed Lottie everywhere, relying on her to direct his movements and behaviour. Joanne had wondered if his reliance on his sister had come about because his parents worked such long hours, both devoted to their careers, so Lottie and Henry had spent a lot of time in childcare since they were a few months old. They were used to their parents working and to being looked after by other people, but she did wonder if he was more attached to Lottie because of it, as she was the one person in his life who was always there. It wasn't that Joanne thought badly of her sister or Jeremy for using childcare, because it was essential with the hours they both worked, but she had a feeling that if she was a mum, she would miss her children terribly and find being away from them for such long periods of time quite difficult.

'Hey there, Henry.' Joanne smiled at her nephew and he grinned up at her, his freckles and ginger hair so much like her own. At three years old, his wrists still carried some of their baby roundness, his button nose cute as a baby's. She pressed a kiss to his head, inhaling the sweet orange scent, no doubt some expensive organic shampoo that Kerry had picked up in a high-street boutique.

'Look at my knee.'

He pointed at the scab and Joanne gasped as if horrified then shook her head. 'Goodness me! How did that happen?'

He told her the story he'd just told her parents about running in the playground at nursery then tripping and his friend, Ben, being very brave and helping him up. Joanne oohed and aahed in all the right places and told him how brave he was, as well as asking if he went to hospital. That made him giggle so she said he should have had a new leg stitched on, which made him laugh even harder and tell her she was a silly billy.

Soon, everyone was in the kitchen and her dad had opened a bottle of wine that he shared between the adults, except for Kerry because she was driving. Joanne had looked at Jeremy from under her lashes, thinking that Kerry had driven last time and it wouldn't hurt him to do it this time, but she also knew that her sister probably had an evening of work ahead of her so wine probably didn't factor into that equation.

She sucked in a deep breath then exhaled slowly, steeling herself for the next hour, hoping she'd hear more from Lottie and Henry than from their parents.

❧

'Ninety-nine . . . one hundred!' Joanne lowered her hands from her eyes. She couldn't believe Lottie had insisted she count to one hundred this time. 'Ready or not, I'm coming!'

She scanned the garden, expecting to see Lottie and Henry straight away but it seemed that their hide-and-seek skills had improved since last time when she'd seen Henry standing behind the bird table and Lottie inside the greenhouse.

She roamed around, peering under trees and behind garden furniture, but couldn't see or hear them. There was only one place left where they could be and that was the shed.

The thought made her shudder.

The shed . . . where she kept some of the stuff. She thought she'd locked it but if her dad had gone in there for something this morning then it could easily have been left open.

Oh no!

She hurried to the bottom of the garden and looked at the wooden construction, built by her dad about eight years ago when the old shed had finally collapsed during a bad storm. The padlock was dangling on the bolt, undone, and the door was open a crack.

From inside came the sound of muffled laughter.

'Lottie! Henry!' She reached for the door and swung it open.

And there they were. Not hiding, but dancing around and giggling, Lottie wearing a floppy white sun hat and crocheted gold shawl and Henry in a red and purple beach kaftan with a pair of giant tortoiseshell designer sunglasses covering most of his face.

'Where did Grandad get all this, Aunty Jo?' Lottie asked, her eyes wide as she turned around. 'There's so many wonderful things.'

'Wonderful thingth,' Henry repeated, his lisp making Joanne's heart flutter even now.

'I . . . uh . . .' Joanne didn't want to fib but knew she was going to have to or her secret would be out, and she didn't think she could trust a five-year-old girl and a three-year-old boy to keep it for her. 'I won them.'

'You won them?' Lottie gasped. 'You must be so lucky. How did you win them?'

'Yes . . .' A voice behind her made Joanne stiffen. 'How on earth did you win all of this?'

Jeremy stepped forwards into the shed and gazed at the piles of boxed shoes, trainers, kitchen appliances, duvet covers in plastic packaging, two games consoles and a flat screen TV, then across at the clothes rail where dresses, shirts, jumpers, skirts and jeans all hung in clear plastic coverings with labels still attached.

'I enter . . . uh . . . a lot of competitions.' Joanne's cheeks burned and she pulled her hair from its ponytail and allowed it to fall forwards to hide her face. She hated blushing and knew that Jeremy would be analysing her, probably seeing right through her fib.

'A lot indeed,' he said as he picked up a set of kitchen utensils in a wooden container and cocked an eyebrow. 'Right, come on children. We need to get going soon. Mum has a pile of paperwork waiting for her and you both need to practise your piano scales.'

The children silently removed the clothing and accessories they'd donned, and Lottie carefully folded them and set them on the wooden floorboards. Joanne thought her heart would melt seeing the young girl being so careful and thoughtful.

'I'll come and see you off,' Joanne said as she pulled the shed door behind her and followed Jeremy and the children back to the house.

She was mortified, aware that Jeremy and Kerry would have plenty to chew over on the journey home, and that she would be the centre of their discussion. They both knew that Joanne didn't earn much, that she was meant to be saving for a house deposit, and that she couldn't possibly have afforded everything she'd stashed in the shed. Therefore, she guessed they'd assume that she either had won it or paid for it with money that wasn't hers.

It was time to do something about her spending habits. Speaking to Roxie and Lila had confirmed it but knowing that her secret had been exposed to her brother-in-law made it even more obvious. Joanne had to take control of the reins of her life and find some sort of order before the chaos swallowed her whole.

4

oodness, Joanne . . . you have been busy.’ Roxie gazed around the spare bedroom at Joanne’s parents’ house, her eyes wide, her mouth open.

‘There’s quite a lot here, isn’t there?’ Lila grimaced.

‘I know . . .’ Joanne’s chest tightened. She’d known this would be difficult but with her parents being out, it had been the right time for her friends to come over. However, now that they were here, she wanted to run to her bedroom, barricade the door and hide under the duvet. The shame was dreadful, exposing herself like this, her inability to avoid an online sale, to ignore the emails that poured into her inbox persuading her to hurry to their website right now or she’d miss the opportunity to get *UP TO 50% OFF*. Why wasn’t she like her friends? Why wasn’t she more like her sister or her frugal parents? She just didn’t have the money to spend and yet she kept on spending it.

Roxie touched her arm gently. ‘Joanne . . . this isn’t the end of the world, you know?’

Joanne blinked. 'Sorry?'

'You don't need to get so upset.'

'Upset?'

Roxie nodded, her eyes filled with concern.

Joanne touched her face and found it was wet. She'd been crying without even realising it.

Roxie slid an arm around her shoulders then hugged her. Initially, Joanne didn't respond, her own emotions were overwhelming her, but Roxie's warmth and her familiar perfume were so comforting that she soon relaxed into the hug and before she knew it, Lila had joined them. The three of them stood that way for a while until Joanne felt calmer, supported, stabilised.

'We'll help you with this.' Roxie stepped back and rested her hands on her hips as she looked around. 'As far as I can see, everything's still boxed up or has the label on it, so it's clear that it's all new and untouched. Is there anything that you'd like to keep, you know, that you really can't bear the thought of parting with before we make a start at listing it all?'

Joanne sniffed then pushed her hair behind her ears. There might be a few things that she should keep for when she could afford her own place, a few things she could use.

'Lila and I will go and make a coffee while you sort out two piles. One that you're keeping and one that's going. But remember, the more you sell on, the more you'll have to pay off some of your debts.'

Ten minutes later, Roxie and Lila were standing in the doorway, mugs in their hands, frowning and shaking their heads.

'Uh . . . Joanne, is that the pile you're keeping?' Lila pointed at the pile on the left that was bigger than the one on the right.

Joanne nodded.

'I . . . uh . . . don't think that's a good idea, do you?' Roxie approached cautiously and looked closer at the largest pile. 'The thing is, Joanne, I meant pick a few things that you absolutely can't bear to part with then the rest can be sold. But looking at that pile you want to keep, you're not going to make much of a dent in things are you?'

'There's more in the shed.' Joanne shrugged, feeling like a petulant teenager.

'Of course, it's up to you . . . but if you want to sort things out properly, you'll have to be more ruthless than that.' Roxie bobbed her head at the larger of the piles.

'Ruthless?' Joanne sighed.

'Ruthless,' Roxie repeated. She went to the pile and picked up a boxed cutlery set. 'You could give this to someone for Christmas or as a wedding gift.'

'I could.' Joanne accepted the cutlery set and clutched it to her chest as if it was the most valuable thing she owned.

'And you could give this to your niece or nephew for a birthday or Christmas.' Lila handed Joanne a box containing a set of junior encyclopaedias.

'You're right.' Joanne nodded, taking the box.

'But if something can't be given to someone you know as a gift, then prepare to let it go.' Roxie picked up a designer handbag. 'Like this . . . it is lovely, but you could sell it for a decent price on eBay. If you list it with a reserve price, I'm sure you could get fifty pounds or more.'

'Okay.' Joanne's heart sank. The cerise and turquoise bag was far too flamboyant and impractical for her to use every day but she'd paid around four hundred for it in a flash sale. The idea of only getting fifty quid was disheartening.

'I know it doesn't sound like much,' Roxie said, putting the bag back down on the pile, 'but it will all help.'

'You're right.' Joanne set the things she was holding down on the floor and rolled up her shirt sleeves. 'I know you're right.'

'How about another coffee then we can go and have a look at what's in the shed too?' Roxie asked, picking up her mug and wiping the lipstick from the rim.

'Good plan.' Joanne swallowed her dread. The bedroom contained a lot less than the shed and she wasn't looking forward to revealing that too, but she also felt a yearning to get it all over and done with so she could feel some relief from the constant sense of dread.

Roxie and Lila led the way downstairs and Joanne followed, wondering what her friends would think when they saw exactly what she'd spent so much money on.

❧

'Next step is the credit cards.' Roxie held up a large kitchen scissors.

'What are you going to do with them?' Joanne tried not to gasp.

They'd spent the morning sorting the bedroom and the shed and Lila had written a list of every item along with a possible price to sell it for on an A4 notepad. It was sensible and practical but Joanne felt herself deflating like an old balloon as the hours wore on. She'd spent so much money buying all these things and for what? She didn't wear them, bake with them, style her hair with them or use them to listen to music. She certainly didn't need most of them and yet she had bought them. It was like an addiction and she wondered, not for the first time, why she felt compelled to buy things.

Was she trying to fill a gap in her life? To distract herself from something?

'It's like you've been trying to comfort yourself, Joanne.' Lila reached across the table and squeezed her hand. 'We've all indulged in retail therapy at some point, and, as you know, I found my own way to comfort myself after Ben left with my . . . nightly performances.'

Joanne smiled in spite of how rubbish she felt. Lila's fiancé had jilted her, and Lila had tried to deal with the pain by dressing up in her wedding dress and accessories every evening and performing karaoke until she was so exhausted she'd collapse into bed. It had taken a trip to the charity shop to get rid of the dress and accessories and a lot of support from her friends to get Lila's life back on track, but here she was, happier than ever.

'Everyone has their coping mechanisms and that's just fine,' Roxie said, waving the scissors as she gesticulated. 'No one knows how they'll cope with a situation until they're in it so do not beat yourself up about this, Joanne. You've used retail therapy as a distraction while others use karaoke, exercise, alcohol, or chocolate. We all cope with things in our own way. The problem is that this is making you miserable and stressing you out and so, therefore, it needs to stop. Destroying the cards will stop you from making things even worse.'

Joanne nodded then stood up and went out into the hallway. Roxie and Lila were right. She took her bag from the under-stairs cupboard and pulled out her purse then returned to the kitchen. Opening her purse, she removed the credit cards and placed them on the table. Roxie handed her the scissors.

'I have to do it?' she asked.

'It has to be you. If I do it you might resent me tomorrow when you can't buy something you see online and we can't have that, can we?' Roxie winked.

Joanne picked up a card and looked at its shiny red and blue plastic surface. It was seemingly innocuous enough, but she knew that it had the power to purchase anything she desired, that it could open new worlds for her and . . . She shook her head. Now she was getting carried away again. This card had a balance of over three thousand pounds and therefore she couldn't justify spending another penny on it. The interest rate alone was crippling her.

'You should also have a look at transferring some balances to a card with a lower interest.' Lila was scanning through her phone. 'There are some good ones on this comparison website that could make a significant impact on the interest you're paying. Some have zero interest on balance transfers for the first three months.'

'That's a really good idea.' Roxie nodded. 'We'll have a look later and make a list of possible cards.'

'But with my credit rating I'll probably get declined.' Joanne winced at her tone, she sounded whiny.

'Worth a shot though,' Lila said.

'Definitely.' Roxie tapped the table. 'Now get cutting.'

Five minutes later, there was a neat pile of plastic on the table. The three women stared at it and Joanne felt as if she'd either giggle hysterically or start crying. It wasn't funny, of course, that she'd accumulated so much debt on the cards, but the sense of relief that she'd started to do something about it was settling over her like a warm, fluffy blanket. Every problem had a solution, even if it wasn't an easy one, and this was the solution to hers. It might take her years to pay everything off, but she would do it and then she'd be able to start saving for a deposit for a house. It would never be a house as grand as Kerry's but at some point in her future she hoped to have a place to call her own, somewhere she could decorate, fill with books and music, with flowers and candles; somewhere she could go when she wanted some time to herself. She could walk around naked, eat ice cream in bed and bake cakes at 2 a.m. if she wanted to. She could . . .

'Walk around naked?' Roxie snorted.

'Sorry?' Joanne frowned.

'You just said you want to be able to walk around naked.'

'Did I?' Joanne winced. She hadn't realised she'd said it out loud. 'I was just thinking about what I'd do if I had a place of my own. Obviously, I can't walk around naked here, can I? Or eat ice cream in bed because Mum gets all anxious if I take food upstairs, although I do sneak some up there sometimes, and if I try to use the oven after seven in the evening, well . . . '

'I can imagine it must be difficult.' Lila offered a smile. 'I'd find it hard not having my own space.'

'I need my own space.' Joanne hugged herself. 'I really do. But I can't have it until I sort my life out, so today is my new beginning. I will stop spending money I don't have so I can eventually start to save some money for my future.'

She felt herself wilting like a flower trapped in the glare of the hot sun even as she said the words.

'What is it?' Roxie tilted her head.

'I know that it's going to take a long time. And I'm thirty-two now. I could be forty or fifty before I'm in a position to so much as rent, let alone buy.'

'Lots of people live with their parents for longer these days,' Roxie said. 'It's different than it used to be because you need such a big deposit to get a mortgage and because unless you're born into money, parents just don't have the means available to help their children out.'

'I know.' Joanne sighed and rubbed her eyes. Just then, she jumped as she heard the front door open. 'Shit! Get rid of these.'

Roxie scooped the cards across the table towards her then tried to brush them into her hand but there was too much plastic and some of it fell to the kitchen floor. She ducked under the table and Joanne and Lila followed but it was only a small table and Lila and Roxie managed to bump heads while Joanne found herself wedged between the chair and the table.

'Goodness me, what's going on here?' Her dad's voice boomed into the kitchen followed by her mum's laughter.

'Well, well . . . is this a game of Twister gone wrong, girls?'

Roxie and Lila crawled out from under the table but not before Roxie had pressed the small pieces of plastic into Joanne's outstretched hands.

'Oh hello, Mr and Mrs Baker.'

'Roxie, dear, no need to be so formal now is there? We've known you for yonks!'

Yonks? Joanne grimaced under the table. How often did you hear that word used?

'Of course, not, ha ha!' Roxie replied as Lila joined her to stand in front of the table. Joanne realised that her friends were providing her with cover to pick up all the pieces of credit cards. 'Hello Hilda and Rex. Been shopping have you?'

While the polite conversation continued, Joanne checked the floor for any stray plastic then stuffed it into her jeans. She hated to be so secretive but the thought of her parents finding out about her debts like this was more than she could bear. It was bad enough that she had lived in Kerry's shadow for so long, let alone have her parents knowing that she had a bad habit of spending money she hadn't earned before she felt prepared to tell them. Disappointing them further than she already had would be truly horrid. If she could just start to make a dent in the debt before she did tell them then it might not be quite so awful.

Crawling out from under the table, she stood up, using the table for balance.

'There you are, Joanne.' Her mum smiled at her as if this type of behaviour was perfectly natural and as if she hadn't known exactly where Joanne was.

'Hi Mum.'

'Whatever were you doing, love?'

'Oh . . . just, uh . . . dropped a biscuit and the crumbs went everywhere. Roxie and Lila were helping me to pick it all up.'

Roxie and Lila fidgeted under her mum's penetrating gaze and Joanne felt like she was ten years old again and she'd been caught licking the icing decorations on top of the Christmas cake. Her mum had always made a Christmas cake and when Joanne and Kerry were younger they'd helped with the cake decorating. That particular year, their mum had taken a class in the art of creating figures and she'd made some beautiful penguins, polar bears and snowmen and women. They had looked so lovely on top of the iced cake that Joanne had been unable to resist tasting them. However, knowing that they would be missed if she removed them from the cake, she'd decided to lick each one and take a nibble from the places she thought wouldn't notice. But one lick and nibble had led to another and before she'd known it, some of the penguins had been missing a wing, the polar bears had been missing feet and the snowmen and women had looked as though they were melting. She'd been desperately trying to repair them when her mum had walked in and caught her. There had been no big drama; an expression of surprise had been followed by her mum calling her dad to the kitchen and then the pair of them had laughed as they'd surveyed the damage. It could have been far worse and Joanne knew that less understanding parents would have reacted differently, but instead, her mum had removed all of the decorations, wiped off the surface of the cake then sat Joanne down at the table for a lesson in creating icing decorations. Her dad had told the story every year over Christmas dinner and every year it had made everyone laugh. But as far as Joanne knew, Kerry had never done anything similar, it had always been Joanne who had the embarrassing stories while Kerry had the achievements.

'What good friends you have,' her dad said as he filled the kettle. 'Cup of tea, girls?'

'Please.' Roxie and Lila nodded and Joanne did too. She didn't know if her parents believed their story but they weren't pushing the issue, so she'd try to relax. Her mum and dad had always been kind and welcoming towards her friends; they were, quite simply, the best parents she could have wished for. It was Joanne who was the problem and sometimes she wished she could be more like Kerry and make them proud of her too.

Perhaps one day she would.

5

A few days later, Joanne let herself out of the house and made her way to the small library. She liked walking around Wisteria Hollow, the Surrey village was so pretty and familiar. She'd left once, years ago, to go travelling, but couldn't imagine leaving again. Having her own home would be lovely but she couldn't envisage living anywhere other than here.

The air was fresh and icy, the clouds sweeping across the sky in the brisk wind and she pulled her coat closer around her throat. There was something really special about dry, crisp autumn days. The air was laced with woodsmoke and other scents, a hint of bacon from someone's breakfast, a waft of coffee as she passed a cottage where the front door was open, and a rich peaty aroma as she passed the churchyard.

Her bag, slung over her shoulder, was heavy with the three hardbacks she'd read in the past two weeks. She'd always been a keen reader but recently she'd found even more comfort in losing herself between the pages of a good book. She also liked visiting the library, there was something soothing about the quiet interior, the way that people moved almost reverently around the old building and spoke only in hushed whispers; how the shelves of books promised so much from fictional adventures of joy and heartbreak to non-fiction prose about visiting distant countries and sampling all sorts of foods.

Joanne had always loved the library, had spent many hours there as a child, especially on rainy Saturdays. Kerry had gone along with her too on occasion and they'd browsed the shelves together, sometimes reaching for the same book, which had made them laugh.

It had been a long time since Kerry had gone to the library but Joanne still went regularly. She had a habit of opening books to read the first page and finding herself still reading several chapters later. Sometimes, she'd realise that her feet were numb, her back aching and her hands chilled as she stood in one of the aisles, a heavy hardback balanced on her arms, the corners digging into her stomach. Time lost all meaning during her library visits.

When she reached the row of stone buildings that housed the village shops, she slowed her pace to peer through the windows, smiling and waving at people she knew inside. At the end of the street was the red-brick building of the library and she paused outside the door to unbutton her coat and to pull off her gloves that she then stuffed into her pockets.

She ran a hand through her windswept hair before pushing open the door and entering. The gentle warmth washed over her immediately along with the familiar aroma of books, a combination of coffee and dark chocolate, along with the slightly more acidic scent of the photocopier which was far less pleasant. It was quiet apart from two elderly men sitting at the computers in the IT area, and a few people milling around the ground floor in the romance and thriller sections.

Joanne went to the desk in the centre of the ground floor and placed the books she was returning on the counter. A woman in front of her wearing a beige wool coat and brown boots sniffed as she waited for the librarian to scan her books. Joanne tried not to stare but her gaze kept returning to the back of woman's head. There was something familiar about the short grey pixie cut.

The woman turned then and caught Joanne's eye.

'Good morning!' she said, smiling.

'Mrs Morris. How are you?'

'I'm well thank you. How're you?'

'I'm good thanks. You're looking well.' Joanne smiled, taking in Freda Morris's rosy cheeks and bright eyes. Joanne knew from Lila that Freda hadn't been well earlier that year, but she seemed to have come through it. Lila was in a relationship with Freda's son and she'd spent a lot of time with Freda since the spring. Joanne knew that the two women had become close, which was nice for Lila because she didn't have any family of her own around.

'Thank you, Joanne. Ethan and Lila have been spoiling me. I'm very lucky.'

Joanne nodded. The relationship between Ethan and Lila had not just been good for them; it had clearly benefitted Freda too.

'There you go, Mrs Morris.' Max Jenkins, the senior librarian, pushed the two paperbacks across the counter to Freda and she took them then placed them inside a cloth tote bag.

'Thank you, Max. I shall let you know how I get on.'

'Please do.'

Joanne watched him leave the counter and go to open the door for Freda then close it gently behind her. While he walked back to the counter, she let her eyes roam over him, from his thick black hair in the quiff that revealed a smooth wide forehead, down his face with incredibly dark brown eyes and to the square jaw with a shadow of stubble. His broad shoulders were evident in a checked shirt and grey jumper and his long muscular legs were shown off in dark denim. He was, quite frankly, one of the best-looking men she'd ever seen. She used to joke with Roxie and Lila that she found Finlay Bridgewater attractive, but although the personal trainer was handsome, he wasn't Joanne's type at all. Plus, since she met Max, she'd developed a soft spot for him.

But however Joanne felt about Max or any other man, she always pushed the feeling away. She had no time or energy for dating or anything more, could never reveal her secret debt to someone else. She'd been aware for some time that getting into a relationship would mean that she'd have to be open and honest about her finances and that thought had turned her cold. And so she'd shut herself off to the opposite sex, declined phone numbers and offers of blind dates (the latter from Kerry and Jeremy who seemed to have a long list of single male acquaintances who were all keen to go on a date with flame-haired Joanne). Why they would want to pair someone up with her she had no idea in light of how she believed they looked down on her, but try they had, to the point where Joanne had had to speak to Kerry privately and ask her to stop. Kerry had seemed shocked but the texts and emails about eligible men she knew had stopped and Joanne had been able to continue her date-free existence.

'Hello Joanne. How're you?' Max smiled at her and she gazed into his big brown eyes framed by square tortoiseshell glasses.

'I'm good, thanks. It's a lovely morning.'

'Indeed it is.' He took the books she placed on the counter and scanned them. 'There you go. Are you taking more out?'

'Yes. I'm going to have a browse around. I saw a few that I fancied last time but tried to limit myself to three.'

'Of course. I know what you mean . . . I'm exactly the same but I figure there's no point in taking out more than one at a time because I'm here five days out of seven.'

Joanne smiled at him, a man who was not only attractive but who liked reading too. He was perfect and probably had a steady partner or his pick of women or men. There was no way that someone like Max would ever fancy her anyway, she thought, so there was no point in allowing herself to think otherwise. Even if she didn't have all the debt to worry about. Even if she'd had the time and energy for dating.

Wandering away from the counter she went to the romance section first, browsing familiar authors, running her fingers along the spines and reading the titles she'd read so many times before. She could probably close her eyes and recite them; she'd visited the library so many times.

She settled on a romantic comedy that had been recently released – and that she was surprised to find on the shelf –

then she headed for the crime and thriller section, keen to locate a gripping page-turner that would be guaranteed to distract her from her worries. Even if she had no money to her name, at least she had the library to turn to, and she could always come here and find more books to read. There was enormous comfort to be found in that.

When she'd selected three titles, she took them to the counter and set them down. Max scanned each book carefully then she tucked them in her bag.

'Good choices.'

'I thought so.'

'We've got a few new titles coming in early next week by the same authors so if you want to put your name down to reserve them you can.'

'It's okay.' She shook her head.

'You sure?'

'Yes. I know it might sound silly, but I don't like to do that in case someone else really wants to read them.'

'You've just as much right as everyone else.'

'I know but I think of some of the elderly people in the village and about some of those who don't have families around and I just couldn't bear to think that I'd taken away something they were looking forward to.'

'That's really sweet of you, you know.'

'Well I don't know about that but—'

'Uh . . . Joanne . . . I don't suppose . . . ' He met her eyes then frowned. 'No . . . probably not.'

'What's wrong?'

A flush crept into his cheeks. 'Nothing. Don't worry about it.'

'Please. If you don't tell me, I'll wonder all day about what you were going to say.'

'Uhhh . . . We've known each other quite a while now, haven't we?'

'Yes. You've been working here for about two years and in the village for longer.'

'I have. And . . . see . . . until just before I got the job here, I was in a relationship with a woman I'd known since we were at university. We didn't live together, obviously, because I moved here and she was living abroad . . . ' He shook his head. 'You don't want to know all this! I'm so sorry. I'm oversharing now . . . But . . . anyway, in brief, I was seeing someone but it's been over a while and I wasn't in a good place to see anyone else. However, lately I've been feeling like it would be nice to go on a date and . . . well . . . '

Joanne held her breath. Was he asking her out? This lovely man who dressed well and liked to read? How could this be happening? What should she do? It was so sweet that he was so shy right now, that he was stumbling over his words, clearly worried about what she thought of him.

'Joanne,' he cleared his throat, 'Would you like to go for a drink?'

She blinked. Exhaled. Coughed.

'You want to go for a drink with me?'

'If you'd like to go out with me.'

His brown eyes held her gaze across the counter. She should say no; it was what she'd told herself many times before. She should walk away with her books and forget this ever happened. She was not in a good position to go out with anyone. Max would likely be horrified if he found out the truth about her debt and run a mile. She didn't know much about him other than the fact that he worked at the library and lived in a small cottage at the other end of the village. He'd inherited it from an aunt who'd passed away years ago and left it almost derelict, so Max had a renovation on his hands when he came to the village. But what else did she know? Any man with any sense would run a mile from her if she disclosed information about her debts to him.

Wouldn't he?

'Yes.' She almost spluttered at her response.

He pushed his glasses up his nose. 'You would?'

'I would. Yes. When?'

Have you lost your mind, Joanne?

'How about tonight?'

'Tonight?' she squeaked.

'Yes.'

'Okay.'

You really have. Decline immediately!

But despite her thoughts, she pulled out her phone and they exchanged numbers.

'Shall I pick you up or shall we meet at The Plough?'

'Let's meet there. No sense in driving when we both live in the village.'

He nodded. 'Wonderful. See you around seven?'

'Seven it is.'

She grinned at him then floated out of the library and onto the cold street, wondering how on earth she'd gone to get books and come away with a date.

For this evening!

With Max.

Gaaaahhhhhhh . . .

She never did anything crazy or spontaneous (apart from online shopping) so this was certainly novel for her. Then another thought struck her and she came down to the pavement with bump.

What the hell was she going to wear?

6

'There's a lovely glow in your cheeks!' Roxie grinned as she let Joanne into her hallway. 'What's happened to you this morning?'

'Oh . . . nothing. I went to the library and came straight here.'

Roxie pouted, her shiny red lips giving her a fifties starlet appeal. 'The library?'

'Yes.'

'And that brought colour to your cheeks?'

'Yes.' Joanne swallowed hard and looked away, knowing that if she met Roxie's curious gaze, her cheeks would burn hotter.

'Take out some raunchy reads did you?' Roxie nudged her.

'No . . . certainly not. I—'

'I'm teasing you, Joanne. Everyone knows that you order erotic romance straight to your Kindle if you want to be discrete about it.' She giggled. 'At least I do but then I always end up reading some of the scenes to Fletcher and . . . ' She sighed. 'Enough said about that I guess.'

Joanne shook her head. It was wonderful to see Roxie so happy after how low she'd been in the summer when she and Fletcher had been having a few issues. Roxie hadn't said much about it, but it had been clear that things weren't as happy as they usually seemed in the Walker household. However, it had all worked out and Roxie and Fletcher were even planning on renewing their wedding vows.

'Something smells incredible.' Joanne sniffed the air appreciatively.

'That would be the raspberry and white chocolate chip muffins.' Roxie gestured towards the kitchen. 'Let's go and have coffee and cake then we can get to work.'

'Sounds good to me.'

Joanne followed Roxie through to the kitchen then sat on one of the tall stools at the kitchen island. Roxie had a lovely home. She'd redecorated many times over the years but it wasn't the décor that made it lovely; it was more that it felt like a home filled with love and laughter, with two people who adored each other and had built a life together. Joanne wondered, not for the first time, what that would be like, but she had no idea if she'd ever find out. The idea of sharing her life with someone did appeal but it would need to be someone she could love and laugh with. But how could she build a life with someone if she couldn't even sort her finances out?

'Where's Glenda?' Joanne looked around for Roxie's small pug. She usually mobbed whoever came to the door, her cute little tail waggling furiously.

'Fletcher has taken her out. He said something about getting her a new bed so chances are that they've gone to one of those large pet warehouses. He'll probably come home with more than a bed. Last time he had about ten packets of treats, three toys and two balls. Our little girl has him wrapped around her paws.'

'That's so sweet.'

Roxie smiled. 'He loves her as much as I do.'

Roxie and Fletcher didn't have any children, but Glenda was like their baby and they spoilt her rotten.

'Latte?' Roxie asked, waving a tall glass mug in front of Joanne.

'Please.'

Roxie pulled some levers on a shiny chrome coffee machine and it made a grinding sound followed by a frothing one then she gave a flick of her wrist above the glass mug. She placed a perfectly created latte topped with a heart in front of Joanne then added a small white china plate with a fat muffin bursting with dark red raspberries and fat white chocolate chips.

When Roxie had made a coffee for herself, she sat opposite Joanne, a muffin in front of her.

'You're just like a professional barista,' Joanne said then she bit into the muffin. 'And mmm. This is delicious.' The tang of the raspberries burst on her tongue followed by the creamy chocolate. 'Where did you learn to make these?'

'Online recipe with one of those YouTube videos. Took me a few attempts to get it just right but as long as you don't overmix the batter, you get perfect muffins.'

'They put mine to shame. I should know better really, working at the café, but I think my problem is that I tend to rush things. I need to learn to take my time. Baking is an art and not to be hurried.' Joanne finished her muffin and licked her fingers.

'Another?' Roxie asked.

'No thanks, tempting as they are.'

'I'll pack three for you to take home.'

'Mum and Dad will appreciate that.' Joanne smiled. 'You know . . . I think I tend to rush most things. It's been my way of distracting myself. If I'm busy, then I don't have time to worry and so I don't take my time to get things right.'

Roxie nodded, her lips pressed together, her hands wrapped around her mug.

'I do have some news actually.'

Roxie leant forwards. 'You do?'

'About why I looked so red when I arrived.'

'Red?' Roxie frowned. 'Oh no, darling, you were glowing.'

'Glowing? I like that.' Joanne chuckled. 'Well . . . at the library . . . you know Max Jenkins?'

'The handsome librarian?'

'That's the one.'

'Yes?'

'He . . . uh . . . asked me out.'

Roxie bounced in her seat. 'He did? That's wonderful news! When are you going?'

'I wasn't going to say yes because I don't think I'm exactly England's most eligible prospect right now.'

'But?'

'But I like him and I answered before I had a chance to decline. It was as if half my brain overrode the other half, impulse over common sense, and before I knew it, I'd accepted. I'm meeting him tonight at seven.'

'Brilliant! I'm so excited for you.' Roxie clapped her hands together sending muffin crumbs flying into the air. One landed in her long dark hair making Joanne think of snowflakes. She pointed at it and Roxie giggled then shook it loose. 'What are you going to wear?'

'We're only meeting at the pub so nothing fancy.'

'But you want to make a bit of an effort, don't you? I mean . . . I can't remember the last date you went on, Joanne.' Roxie gazed into the distance as if trying to think of a time when Joanne had gone out.

'It was ages ago. I'm so out of practice and incredibly rusty. It'll probably be a complete disaster and he'll never want to see me again.'

Roxie reached across the island and squeezed Joanne's hand. 'Look, lovely, don't put so much pressure on yourself. You might not have dated anyone in a long time but that's because you've been busy and you don't want to just settle for anyone. This evening will be fun, you'll see. Think of it as meeting a friend for a drink. Don't have any expectations before you go and don't be negative about yourself. Max clearly likes you or he wouldn't have asked you out. And why wouldn't he like you? You're intelligent, funny, warm, kind, and beautiful.'

'And massively in debt.'

Roxie waved a hand dismissively. 'We're sorting that out and there's no need to share that with him anyway. It's a date not a marriage proposal so the finer details of your finances are on a strictly need to know basis and he doesn't need to know. If things work out between you, you'll have sorted everything out by then and not have to worry about telling him about the plastic cards you hammered.'

'Hammered?' Joanne snorted. Even when Roxie was being kind she could throw in some humour.

'Your little plastic friends did take a hammering but you're on the up now. So . . . back to what you're wearing. Let's have a look through the list of purchases and see if we can put an outfit together.'

Ten minutes later, Roxie and Joanne had decided upon a navy jumpsuit with a tiny sunflower print and a pair of navy pumps. Roxie had said that with Joanne's red hair, it would look wonderful and Joanne hoped she was right. Joanne was grateful for Roxie's fashion advice because if she'd had to decide on something herself it would probably have been jeans and a T-shirt. Nothing wrong with that but Roxie had spoken to her about how the right clothes could boost her confidence. It would remain to be seen when she tried it on later, but she could hope.

'We have to remove it from the list of items to sell because you're keeping it.' Roxie scribbled out the jumpsuit and pumps on the A4 lined paper. 'But it doesn't matter because you still have plenty on there.'

Joanne nodded. She certainly did.

'Right, off to the study we go!'

Roxie headed out of the kitchen and up the stairs and Joanne followed her, casting a glance at the remaining muffins on the wire rack, wishing she could stuff another one into her mouth and enjoy the sweet fluffy comfort they offered, but knowing that the sooner they got the items listed on eBay, the sooner people could start to bid on them.

After they'd finished, Joanne popped home to drop off the muffins and to pick up the outfit. Roxie had said she'd help her get ready and Joanne knew that she could use some help. Plus, the idea of getting ready alone made her stomach churn because her nerves were building, so she hoped Roxie would help to distract her.

'Ooh muffins!' her mum said as she removed the lid from the Tupperware tub.

'Roxie sent them over.'

'She's very kind. We can have them for breakfast tomorrow if your dad doesn't get to them first.'

Joanne smiled. Her dad certainly had a sweet tooth and many a time her mum had reached for a biscuit to have with her morning cuppa, only to find that her dad had finished off the packet watching TV the night before.

'Hide them well!' Joanne walked to the kitchen door. 'By the way . . . I'm going out tonight so I'm going to grab a few things then head back to Roxie's.'

'Going out?' Her mum sounded surprised. 'Where?'

'Just to the pub.'

'With the girls?'

Joanne cleared her throat. The last thing she wanted to do was to fib to her mum but she also didn't want to tell her that she had a date. Her mum would get all excited or overly concerned then there would be more pressure and she'd want to know how it went. Also, she'd probably tell Kerry who would then tell Jeremy and soon her whole family would know and ask a million questions. For now, she wanted to keep it to herself.

And Roxie, of course.

She was about to say something vague about who she was meeting but her mum was already digging around in the freezer, no doubt looking for something for dinner. She had a habit of making huge slow cooker pots of casserole and curry, soup and Bolognese, so she always had plenty left over to freeze.

'Will you be here for dinner?' Her mum turned around holding a freezer bag containing one of her signature dishes.

'I don't think so. I'll eat when I'm out. What're you having?'

Her mum peered at the bag, raised it to the window to see it better in the light then shrugged. 'I forgot to label it so it's a surprise. Looks like casserole or Bolognese though, so I'll need to toss a coin on whether to do pasta or mash.'

'Pasta will go with either one.' Joanne nodded. 'Although you could probably get away with mash too.'

Her mum placed the frozen dinner down on the worktop then wiped her hands on a towel. 'You're right and seeing as how there's a football documentary on TV later, your dad won't notice anyway. I could feed him apple tart covered with instant gravy and he wouldn't notice if he's engrossed in the TV.'

Joanne knew her mum was right. Her parents did have quite traditional roles in a lot of ways with her mum cooking meals, doing the washing and ironing and her dad taking care of the car, decorating and doing most of the driving, but it worked for them. Joanne wouldn't want a relationship with more traditional roles because she didn't like the idea of always being the one deciding what to have to eat (all that pressure!) and she loathed ironing. She had always imagined that if she did find a soulmate then they'd share things equally without either of them having concrete roles. Her mum and dad were good friends, they loved each other, took care of each other and they were happy, even after many years together. If she could find someone who made her as happy as her dad made her mum and vice versa, then she'd feel very lucky indeed.

'You enjoy your dinner and your evening and I'll see you later.' Joanne hugged her mum then went upstairs to get her outfit and what little make-up she possessed. Catching sight of herself in the mirror with her hair wild from being outside in the wind and her nose pink from the cold, she thought she was going to need all the help she could get to be date ready. She had to hope Roxie could work some magic.

7

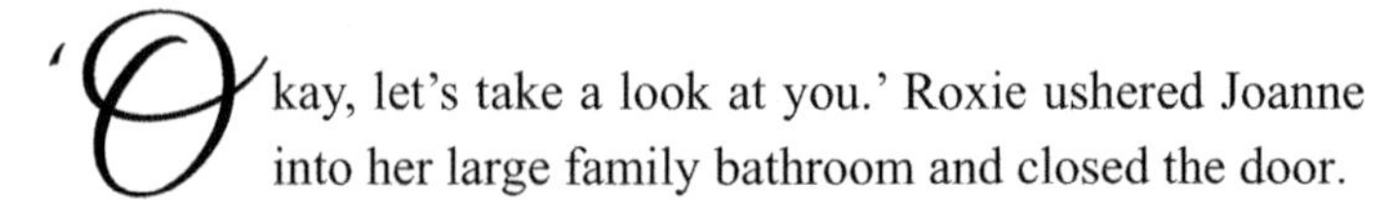

‘Okay, let’s take a look at you.’ Roxie ushered Joanne into her large family bathroom and closed the door.

‘Why have you closed that? It’s only us two here.’

‘I know but I thought you’d like some privacy anyway for what we’re about to do.’

‘Just what are we planning on doing here?’ Joanne asked, unease making her conscious of how warm she was in the fluffy white dressing gown Roxie had given her to wear while she administered some beauty treatments.

‘Just a bit of a tidy up, a dash of highlighter here and there and some serum to show off that gorgeous hair.’

‘A tidy up of what?’ Joanne tightened the belt of the dressing gown.

‘Nothing below the waist, don’t worry.’ Roxie rooted around in a make-up bag then pulled out tweezers.

‘Where then?’

'Sit on the toilet lid and I can tidy up those brows.'

'Roxie, I like my eyebrows as they are.'

'So do I . . . they're lovely, perfect in fact, but there are a few strays . . . '

Roxie placed a hand on Joanne's head and tilted it back. Joanne closed her eyes as the tweezers approached. With each hair that Roxie plucked, Joanne winced and yelped, the pain was like being prodded with hot needles.

'Joanne, don't be such a baby.'

'A baby? You're torturing me.' She tried to move her head but Roxie had her pinned in place.

'I know your eyebrows are fair but there are quite a few stragglers underneath and above your nose and you don't want to go on a date with a monobrow now do you?'

Joanne opened one eye. 'A monobrow? Since when do I have a monobrow?'

'Not anymore!' Roxie stood back and grinned. 'That's better. Much tidier.'

Joanne stood up and looked in the mirror above the sink. She couldn't see much difference except for that fact that the skin underneath her eyebrows was red and looked a bit swollen.

'Now . . . next on the list is that top lip.'

Joanne covered her mouth. 'What's wrong with my top lip?'

'You've a few blonde hairs there that keep catching the light.'

'I'll sit in the dark.'

'In the pub?'

'Yes.'

'But if it's one of those corner tables in the pub then the candlelight will make those babies glow.'

'Babies?'

'Little golden hairs. Let's get some cream on them and you'll soon be smooth and hairless.'

'Dear god, Roxie, that doesn't sound right.'

'I meant your upper lip.'

'I know but this is all rather dramatic isn't it? If I look that bad then why did he ask me out?'

'No one said you look bad, darling, but you're polishing what you have to make it shine. Can you trust me?'

She held Joanne's gaze and all Joanne could see in her eyes was love and concern. Roxie was a good friend and she genuinely wanted to help. What did it matter if Joanne had to go through a few 'pampering' treatments? She was lucky to have a friend like Roxie who cared enough to help her in this way.

'Of course, I trust you. Do what needs to be done.'

Joanne sat back on the toilet lid and closed her eyes then Roxie got back to work. Her fingers were light as they touched Joanne's skin and her perfume, a heady scent with notes of jasmine and rose, was familiar and comforting.

Joanne felt herself relaxing and soon she was floating, hovering on the edge between consciousness and awareness, while her friend looked after her and it was a wonderful place to be.

❧

'Keep your eyes closed.' Roxie led Joanne along the landing and into a room where the carpet was so plush it made her feel unsteady even though her new navy pumps were flat. 'Hold on a moment . . .'

Roxie gently turned Joanne around.

'Well, what do you think?'

Opening her eyes slowly, Joanne found herself in Roxie's bedroom in front of a full-length mirror staring at a woman she barely recognised. The navy jumpsuit fitted her curves like a second skin, the pumps matched perfectly and her face was flawless. She stepped closer and peered at her reflection, raising a hand to touch her cheek.

'Is that really me?' she squeaked, stunned at the transformation.

Roxie had washed and conditioned her hair with a treatment then rubbed a clear serum through it, blow-dried it and wrapped it around fat Velcro rollers before setting the drier over them. She'd left the rollers in for an hour while she'd done Joanne's make-up then gently unrolled them and run her fingers through Joanne's hair. The result was soft bouncy red waves that made Joanne think of glamorous celebs on the covers of glossy magazines. Roxie had also done an amazing job with her make-up, using a tinted moisturiser as a base, a peachy blusher on her cheeks then highlighted her cheekbones and nose before creating a smoky eye effect with grey and silver eyeshadow. She'd finished with mascara and a pink lip gloss that made Joanne's lips look plump and kissable.

'It's you all right.' Roxie squeezed her shoulder. 'The basics were already there. I just added a touch of polish.'

'I'm really impressed.' Joanne touched her hair, amazed by how bouncy it felt. 'But I'm also a bit worried.'

'Why are you worried? Max is going to be very impressed.'

'He also might not recognise me or worse, he could think I've gone to a lot of trouble for a date and therefore think I'm desperate.'

Roxie laughed then, throwing back her head and closing her eyes.

'No he won't. He'll be thanking his lucky stars and thinking how hot you are.'

'If you say so.'

Joanne turned sideways and gazed at her reflection, admiring the jumpsuit and how her hair shone as it caught the light.

'Now . . . let's go and have a little aperitif before you get going.'

Roxie took Joanne's hand and led her downstairs to the kitchen where she took two tumblers from the cupboard and set about making them a drink. Joanne sat at the kitchen island taking care not to crease her clothing and watched as Roxie made them gin and tonics.

When Roxie handed her a drink, Joanne took a sip and her tongue tingled at the zesty tonic then the gin warmed her blood and she started to relax. This evening was her first date in what felt like a lifetime, but she was looking forward to it, and thanks to her wonderful friend, she felt confident enough to go and enjoy it too.

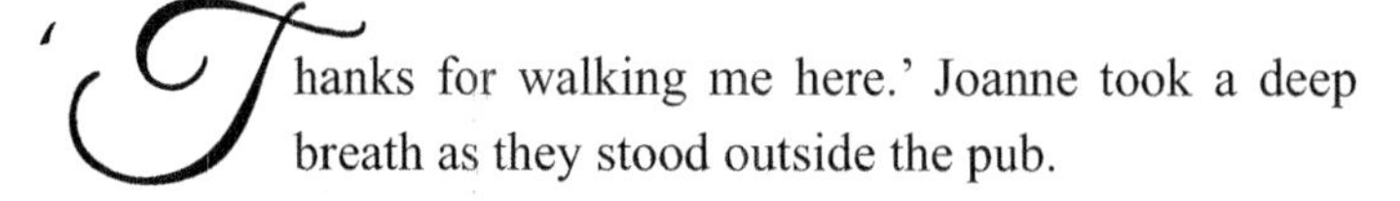

'Thanks for walking me here.' Joanne took a deep breath as they stood outside the pub.

'No problem. To be honest, Joanne, you seem so nervous I was worried that if I didn't, you might not come.'

Joanne gulped. 'I am nervous but I wouldn't have stood Max up. He's such a nice person.'

'I'm glad to hear that. I'd hate for you to miss out on what could well be an enjoyable evening.'

'Gosh I hope it's going to be enjoyable. Okay . . . here goes.'

'Good luck!' Roxie kissed her cheek then nudged Joanne towards the doors.

Joanne pushed on the door but it wouldn't budge. She tried again and turned to Roxie in confusion. 'It's locked.' Had she got the time wrong? Had the pub closed down and she'd missed it? Where would Max be?

'You have to *pull* the door, Joanne.' Roxie stood on the pavement with her hands on her hips.

'I'm so stupid sometimes.' Joanne shook her head, turned back to the door and pulled it open. She waved at Roxie then went inside.

The smell that washed over her was familiar: chips, vinegar, beer, coffee. There were other layers too: a hint of woodsmoke, tones of rose and jasmine, cedarwood and citrus.

After removing her coat and scarf, she stood there for a moment, looking around, then caught sight of Max at the bar. She gazed at him, her heart fluttering. With his thick dark hair, glasses and broad shoulders he was gorgeous. He was wearing faded denim jeans and a grey shirt. He turned as if sensing her watching him and smiled. Her nerves drifted away. He was a warm and friendly man and she knew she could make conversation with him from the chats they'd had, so what was there to be nervous about?

'Hello.' He smiled at her when she arrived at the bar. 'You look lovely, Joanne.'

'Really?' she asked, looking down at herself as if to check what she was wearing.

'The jumpsuit is cool and your hair looks gorgeous.'

'Does it?' She watched his face as if evaluating his honesty.

'Yes of course.' He tilted his head. 'You're not very good at accepting compliments, are you?'

Joanne lowered her eyes to her feet to break eye contact for a moment. Max's gaze was so intense, his dark brown eyes almost black, his face so handsome that she was feeling a trifle warm. She'd always been sensitive but able to push things away. Take yoga, for instance, her friends often commented on how laid-back she seemed during classes, especially the times when she'd fallen asleep or broken wind in one of the more challenging poses. She'd brushed these things off as if they didn't bother her, but sometimes, deep down, they did. She'd never wanted to seem self-obsessed or self-pitying or anything like that and so it was easier to focus on others and what they were doing, what they might be thinking or feeling, without allowing herself to feel self-conscious. If she analysed it in enough detail, she knew she'd probably find that it went back to Kerry and how she'd always felt that she was in her older sister's shadow, how she'd wished she could be that intelligent, cool, successful, stylish and strong. Since they were children, she'd looked up to Kerry and they'd been close, but then, as teenagers, Kerry had broken away. By the time they were adults, Kerry had seemed aloof, from a different class to Joanne and so she'd swallowed her sadness and tried not to mind. But sometimes it did hurt and she missed her close relationship with her sister terribly.

'Joanne?' It was Max, peering at her, his eyes filled with concern.

'Yes?' She blinked.

'Are you okay?'

'Yes, why?'

'I asked what you'd like to drink.'

'Oh . . . sorry. Uh . . . I'll have a glass of red wine please.'

'Which one?' He gestured at the bar behind him and the young woman behind the bar stepped aside for Joanne to read the wine list on the chalkboard.

Joanne read the names, realising that she didn't know that much about some of them and didn't want to pick an expensive one seeing as how Max was paying for this round. Also, she'd have to get the next round, so an expensive one was beyond her means seeing as how she was meant to be cutting her spending and paying off debts.

'The house red is lovely,' the woman behind the bar said. 'It's very easy-drinking.'

'I'll have a glass of that then please.' Joanne smiled her gratitude at the woman for coming to her rescue.

'I'll have the same.' Max pulled a wallet from his pocket. 'Make them large.'

Joanne swallowed. She'd have to take her time. The gin and tonic she'd had with Roxie had eased her nerves for a while but the fresh air on the walk here had diminished the effects of the alcohol. However, here in the warm, with the relaxed atmosphere and the excitement of being on a date, she knew that she'd be more affected by alcohol and the last thing she wanted was to get drunk and show herself up.

'There you go.' Max handed her a glass of wine and Joanne stared at it. The glass could have held three goldfish easily. The wine only came halfway up though, so that was a good thing as she suspected that if filled to the brim, it would hold a full bottle.

'Thanks. Shall we grab a table?'

'Near the fire?'

'Good plan.'

They headed across the bar and took the closest table to the fireplace. Joanne sat on the bench with the tall back, settling into cushions with red covers embroidered with gold thread that reminded her of the cushions in a church. She set her bag on the floor under the table and placed her coat next to her. Max placed his wine on the small round table then sat on a chair opposite, hanging his own coat over the back.

Joanne raised her glass. 'To a good evening.'

'Cheers.' He gently clinked his glass against hers then drank while Joanne did the same.

She swallowed the wine then took another sip. It was delicious, fruity and spicy with aromas of blackberries and cinnamon.

'That is a good wine.'

'Very nice. Good choice.'

'I didn't really choose it, did I?'

'Yes, you did.' He frowned.

'Well . . . with the barmaid's help.'

'Taylor.' He nodded. 'She knows her wine. Married to a wine rep.'

'That's her name! I know it's awful, but I always forget whether it's Taylor or Tania. I guess it's probably because I don't come in here that often.'

Max laughed. 'Perhaps you need to come here regularly then. After all, it's not fair on Taylor to have her name forgotten.'

'So true!' Joanne giggled. 'Very remiss of me.'

They both sipped their wine and Joanne felt it warming her belly, seeping into her veins and relaxing her. At their side, the fire crackled in the grate, sparks flying up the chimney as pine cones nestled in with the logs popped and rosemary twigs sent their woody, herbal scent into the air.

'Are you hungry? Max asked.

'I'm always hungry.'

'Me too.'

He handed her a menu from the stand on the table and took one for himself.

Joanne looked at the prices first, working out what would be the best value and settled on lasagne and chips with garlic bread. It might not be the most romantic of foods as it would be heavy with garlic but she wasn't expecting to be kissed this evening so guessed it didn't really matter. Plus, at less than ten pounds, it was about as cheap as she could get without just having a starter and a dessert.

'Know what you want?' Max asked after five minutes. 'I think I'll have a burger.'

'Yes, thanks. I'll go and order.' She reached for her bag.

'No, no.' He shook his head. 'Easier for me to go as I'm closer to the bar.'

'What? That doesn't matter and I'm hardly miles away.'

'Please. Let me.' He stood up. 'My treat.'

'No, Max, I can't let you do that.'

'Look . . . I don't want to be presumptuous here but perhaps you could get the next meal.'

'The next meal?'

'If you enjoy this evening, you could get the meal the next time we go out.'

'Oh!' A tingling spread through her making goosebumps stand up on her arms. 'Okay.'

'Great.' He grinned then went to the bar.

Joanne fingered the stem of her wine glass, playing what had just happened over in her mind. They'd only been here twenty minutes and already he was thinking about seeing her again. It was unexpected and she'd not really dared to think beyond this evening, but it seemed that Max already had some idea about how he felt. Of course, she shouldn't let herself get carried away; this was just a date and they had a few hours to go yet, so things could go horribly wrong in that time and . . .

Joanne! Stop it. Just be here in the moment and enjoy yourself.

She sucked in a breath then blew it out hard before pushing her shoulders back then she ran her fingers through her soft hair. There was no point being negative when the evening had only just begun.

Raising her glass to her lips, she sipped the wine, allowing it to slide over her tongue, savouring the flavours. It was good and would go well with her choice of food.

The doors to the pub opened sending a gust of chilly air into the room. A familiar face grinned at her and winked. Roxie had clearly decided to come and offer moral support. Fletcher was with her and he waved at Joanne, looking a bit sheepish she thought, as if Roxie had forced him to come to the pub against his better judgement. Roxie pointed at the bar then at a table near the door and Joanne nodded. Her friend would be there if she needed her and she was grateful for that.

As Fletcher took his wife's coat, Joanne couldn't help smiling. Roxie looked amazing as always in skinny black jeans, long brown boots and a sparkly top that exposed one toned shoulder. Her dark hair softly waved so it bounced around her shoulders. As they walked to the bar, Fletcher's eyes were fixed on his wife, and not for the first time, Joanne found herself wishing that someone would look at her that way. Even just once.

❧

'That was delicious. Thank you so much.' Joanne wiped her mouth with a napkin then finished her wine. The lasagne had been rich and garlicky, the bread crusty and buttery, the chips fat and fluffy on the inside.

'My pleasure, Joanne.' Max swept a chip around his plate, clearing up the barbecue sauce that had come with his burger, then he wiped his hands on his napkin. 'I really enjoyed it too.'

Their food had arrived within half an hour of ordering and in that time they'd chatted about their days and the weather forecast for the next month – it was meant to get a lot colder – about their jobs and weekend plans. Max would be working the following day as the library opened on Saturday mornings but he was going to a friend's on Sunday for lunch. The friend who was married with two young children didn't live in the village. He often invited Max for dinner and Max joked that he thought it was because they took pity on him as one of their only single friends.

'Fancy another drink?' she asked.

'That would be lovely and shall we look at desserts?'

'Uh . . . ' Joanne actually felt quite full but dessert sounded tempting.

'What about sharing one?'

'All right.'

'They have churros and they're always nice.'

'Sure. I'll just pop to the loo first then order on my way back.'

'But this evening's meant to be my treat.'

'How about if I get dessert this time then next time I'll pay for the main course and you can get the dessert?'

'Good plan.'

She picked up their glasses and carried them to the bar, her heart fluttering with pleasure at the thought of another evening like this.

She was washing her hands when the door opened and Roxie came in.

'Hello there!' Roxie sashayed to her side and wrapped an arm around her shoulders then met her eyes in the mirror above the sink. 'How's it going? Fletcher and I have been on tenterhooks.'

'Tenterhooks?'

'Joanne, really? It means that we've been tense, hoping it's going well. But judging from the way you kept laughing and gazing into each other's eyes, it's going extremely well.'

'It is actually.' Joanne smiled at their reflections. 'I'm having fun.'

'I am so glad to hear that. He's as nice as we thought then?'

'Very sweet and attentive and . . . I'm not sure if this makes sense but it's like I can see a kindred spirit in him.'

'In what way?'

'Not to make him sound like a sad case or anything, but I think he's been a bit lonely too and he understands how it feels to want the chance to enjoy the company of someone who gets that.'

'Wow, you two are making progress. Kindred spirits as well.' Roxie hugged her with one arm. 'I'm delighted. But seriously, Joanne, he looks like he's into you. I don't think this is just because he's lonely or those huge glasses of wine you were drinking. He can't take his eyes off you.'

'Really?'

'Yes. So get back out there and have another drink.'

'I will. And we're having dessert.'

'Excellent!' Roxie opened her purse. 'And if that's the case then things could progress further so . . . just in case, I'm going to get you something.' She went to the two machines fixed to the wall next to the mirror and took out a few coins.

'I don't need tampons, Roxie.'

'Not tampons, darling.' Roxie giggled. 'Protection.'

The coins clinked as Roxie pushed them through the slot then she pressed a button and there was a clunk as something landed in the open tray at the bottom of the machine. She took it out and brought it over to Joanne. 'Just in case.'

'What is it?' Joanne peered at the box. '*Roxie!* I don't need these.'

'Just in case, darling. It would be far worse to have need of them and not have any with you.'

'But I'm going home afterwards.'

Roxie shrugged. 'As I said, just in case.'

Joanne reached for her bag to stuff the box of condoms into it but realised she'd left in under the table. 'I don't have anywhere to put them.'

'Here.' Roxie took the small square box then pulled down the shoulder of Joanne's jumpsuit and tucked it into her bra strap. 'Just pop it into your bag when you get back to the table.'

'Okay.' Joanne wished she could throw the box away immediately but she knew Roxie was being helpful and didn't want to offend her, so instead she pulled the jumpsuit back into place and looked at her reflection. The box was small and couldn't really be seen under the material so hopefully she would get away with it. Although she knew, one hundred percent, that she would not be needing condoms tonight. The idea was ridiculous, laughable, preposterous . . .

And yet, as she walked back through to the bar, she wondered for a moment what it would be like to kiss Max's full lips, to feel his arms around her and to give in to desire. It wasn't something she'd done very often in her thirty-two years. Perhaps it was the wine, good food and enjoyable company, but the thought of being with Max was more than a little bit appealing.

'I forgot my purse,' Joanne said when she arrived back at the table.

Max looked up at her. 'I can pay.'

'No, it's fine, honestly. Could you grab my bag for me, please? It's under the table.'

He pushed his chair back, leant forwards and reached for her bag then handed it to her. She saw that the table had already been cleared of their plates and cutlery.

'Won't be long.'

He nodded.

At the bar, she ordered dessert then another two large glasses of wine. While Taylor poured the drinks, Joanne looked around the bar. She saw a few familiar faces and some she didn't know and then there was Roxie. Giving her a double thumbs up from where she was sitting with Fletcher. He was reading the menu, or rather hiding his face with it, so Joanne suspected that he was finding his wife's behaviour a bit embarrassing. But, like Joanne, he would know that it was simply because Roxie had her friend's best interests at heart and because Roxie just wanted to see everyone happy. She'd already helped Joanne so much over the years that she would never feel anything other than grateful for having Roxie in her life. She was one of the most loving and compassionate people Joanne had ever met and she knew that Lila felt the same about Roxie because she'd been there for her too.

Taylor set the wine in front of Joanne and she paid then carried the glasses over to their table. 'Taylor said dessert will be about ten minutes.'

'Sounds good to me.' Max rubbed his stomach. 'Give the burger time to move down a bit.'

'What time do you start tomorrow?'

'Eight thirty but I like to get in by eight so I've time for a coffee and to get everything ready before the hordes arrive.'

'Hordes?'

He laughed. 'Lots of enthusiastic book borrowers about at the weekend.'

'More than in the week?'

'It's mainly those who work Monday to Friday. I'm lucky to be able to keep the library running really because some villages have lost theirs.'

'It would be dreadful to lose the library. As with the shops, pubs and the village hall, it's an integral part of the community.'

'My thoughts exactly. Plus, it's my job.'

'Did you always want to be a librarian?'

A small line appeared between his brows. 'Not as a child. Back then I used to want to be a pilot or a soldier or a truck driver.'

'Goodness!'

'I know, stereotypes or what? It was as I got older and realised how much I loved reading that I knew I wanted to work with books, whether as a librarian, writer or bookseller. I even considered editorial work and publishing at one point.'

'What changed your mind about a career in publishing?'

He took a sip of wine. 'I did a degree in English literature with creative writing and spent a summer at a publishing office in London. Seeing the sheer amount of work that it entailed along with the commutes that many of the employees made every day put me off. I love London but realised I wouldn't want to be there every day. I'm more of a rural village person. I like long walks, fresh air, and a short commute to work. You know, all those simple things that make life easier.'

'I can understand that. So you decided on being a librarian?'

'I really enjoy my job and I've worked in other libraries over the years. However . . . ' He toyed with a beer mat and raised one eyebrow slowly. 'If I tell you something do you promise you won't laugh?'

'Of course.'

'I like to write.'

'Write what?'

'It kind of started with book blogging. I was reading so many good books that I wanted to share them with others. Via that I was in contact with lots of authors and publishers and that led me to wonder if it was worth me trying to write a book myself.'

'How exciting!' Joanne gazed at him in awe. He was bright, she knew that, but also talented. *Writing a book!*

He cleared his throat. 'Not that exciting because I tried a few times and ended up scrapping what I'd written. But a few of the authors who became friends told me not to give up. They said it always takes a few tries to find your author voice, your style and so on and that I should keep trying.'

'How did you get on?'

A smile played on his lips. 'I've finished one draft of a spy thriller and I'm quite pleased with it.'

'I'd love to read it.'

His cheeks turned pink and he rubbed at the back of his neck.

'Maybe one day. See . . . It's a very rough draft at the moment so I need to edit it and develop it, but then I've plans for two more in the series. When I've written them, I'll send them to an agent.'

'A literary agent?'

He bobbed his head. 'I've done some research and know a few I'd like to submit to so when I do, we'll see if it's any good.'

'Are they all looking for the same thing then?'

He shook his head. 'I've been told it's a very subjective business and that if one agent rejects my work then to try another. In fact, I've been told to keep trying until I find one who likes my work and who seems a good fit.'

'That's fascinating and very exciting. Couldn't you send the first book and see what they think while you write the next?'

'I could and I've debated what's best to do. I could even send the first along with synopses for the other two, I guess. That would be one way to show that I've more than one book in me.'

'Do you have lots of ideas then?'

'Hundreds.' He laughed. 'My house is full of notebooks. I have one in every room in case inspiration strikes and piles of them in my lounge and study and they're all filled with notes about plots and characters.'

'Oh I hope you find an agent and get a publishing deal.' Joanne felt a prickle of emotion in her throat. Max's whole face had lit up as he spoke about his writing and it was clear that being published would be a dream come true for him.

'Thank you. But even if I don't go through the traditional publishing model, I'll try another route. I also know several hybrid authors who are doing well.'

'What's a hybrid author?'

'Someone who is published with a publisher and who self-publishes. A lot of authors do it these days. It means that they have a variety of ways to earn and pursue their careers.'

'Well here's to being published.' Joanne held up her glass. 'Wishing you every success with following your dreams. Who knows, in a year or two you could be signing books at the library.'

'Now wouldn't that be something?' He laughed. 'I can't imagine it will happen that quickly but it's nice to have dreams. Besides which, I'm really enjoying writing at the moment. There's no pressure on me at all in terms of deadlines and I can write at my own pace. I've heard that deadlines can add a fair bit of pressure, but can also be motivating.'

Taylor arrived at their table with a rectangular dish that she set down on the table. 'Your churros. Enjoy. Can I get you anything else?'

Joanne looked at her glass and was surprised to find it was almost empty.

'Another wine?' Max asked.

'I probably shouldn't.'

'One more won't hurt will it? We'll need something to wash these down.' He gestured at the dish.

'Okay then. Twist my arm.' Joanne giggled, aware that she was feeling a bit tipsy.

'Two more wines coming right up.' Taylor took their empty glasses then walked away.

'What about you, Joanne?' he asked. 'Do you like your job?'

'I do.' She smiled as she thought about the lovely atmosphere at the cafe. 'I like how I get to speak to people all day long and how busy it is there.'

'Did you ever want to do anything else?'

She gave a wry laugh. 'As a child perhaps but I can't even remember what it might have been. I left the village after the first year of my A levels to go travelling, found that I missed home terribly, came back and haven't left since. As far as jobs go, I've done a variety of things including some admin, but working at the cafe has been the only thing I've really liked. I don't know if it will be the job I always have but at the moment I still feel like I'm not sure what I want to do. I guess that sounds pathetic, right?'

'Not at all. If you're happy as you are then why change things?'

He was so understanding, not at all judgmental, and Joanne realised that she liked him more and more as the evening wore on.

She looked down at the churros and her mouth watered. The piped doughnuts were crisp and golden and there was a pot of shiny chocolate dipping sauce at the side.

'Shall we get stuck in?' Max asked. 'I don't know about you but I can't wait to try one.'

'Nor me.' Joanne picked up a churro and dipped it in the sauce. When she put it in her mouth, she moaned. 'That is so good.'

Max copied her actions then his eyes widened. 'Yum.'

'Better than sex.' Joanne started as she realised what she'd said. 'Uh. . . I didn't mean to say that. It must be the wine.'

Max grinned at her. 'I'm not sure I can agree with the better than sex bit, but I guess it depends who you're doing it with.'

Joanne's cheeks flushed. She didn't have many experiences to compare it to but when it came down to good food or sex, she'd have to think carefully about it. Perhaps Max was right though; perhaps it would be better with the right person.

The right person?

Was there even such a thing or was that just something peddled by romance authors and film directors? By card companies trying to sell Valentine's cards and florists wanting to sell flowers? By jewellers who dealt in engagement rings and by wedding planners? Joanne's experience of romance was limited, her belief in true love so stale after years of disappointments that she wouldn't even like to indulge the idea that sex and relationships could be anything other than frustrating. For other people it might be better than dessert, yes, but not for her.

She stuffed another churro into her mouth and chewed.

'You like them?' Max asked.

'They're delicious.' She licked her fingers.

When she looked down at the dish, she gasped. There were only two left which meant that they'd eaten seven each already. So much for taking her time.

'Do you want to order some more?' he asked as Taylor brought them fresh glasses of wine.

'Oh . . . no, I'm fine thanks.'

'No problem.'

When they'd emptied the dish, Joanne sat back and sighed. 'That was so good. Thank you.'

'You got them.'

'I meant the evening and the company.'

He gazed at her for a moment then he leant forwards. 'Come here.'

'Pardon?'

'Come closer.'

She moved towards him, her heart thundering as rested her elbows on the table. He leant closer, reaching out to her. Was he going to kiss her? Here and now? He took her face in his hands and she sighed. His hands were soft and warm on her skin, his eyes so dark she felt like she could sink into them and her whole body tingled with anticipation.

As he got closer, she closed her eyes and waited to feel his lips on hers.

And waited.

She thought perhaps he was struggling to reach her, so she pushed herself up off her seat and moved closer to him, her eyes still closed. She wanted this, so much, more than she could recall ever wanting to be kissed.

And then, the brush of his thumb over her bottom lip and at the corner of her mouth made her gasp.

But the kiss didn't come.

She opened her eyes and found Max staring at her curiously.

Their faces just inches apart.

He was smiling but didn't look as if he wanted to kiss her. There was no desire in his eyes, no flush to his cheeks. He looked, quite frankly, a bit surprised.

She looked down and saw that she was leaning quite far over the table which meant that her not insignificant cleavage was pressing against the neckline of her jumpsuit and that had caused the shoulders to tighten too. Gravity was taking control and she had to move backwards or fall face down on the table.

She pushed herself backwards and as she did so, the straining at her neckline stopped. There was a twang as her bra strap snapped back against her skin and something popped out and flew through the air. Max ducked and it sailed past his head and onto the tiles in front of the hearth.

Joanne slumped in her seat, her head hazy with wine. A mixture of disappointment at not being kissed and embarrassment at shooting the box of condoms at her date swirled through her.

Max went to the fireplace and picked up the box. As he turned around, Joanne could see amusement and surprise on his features and she willed the floor to open up and swallow her whole. Bloody Roxie and her great ideas. Now Max would think she had expected him to kiss her and more.

He returned to the table.

'Uh . . . sorry about that, Joanne. You had chocolate sauce on your lip and stuck in the corner and I was just wiping it away. But . . . uh . . . I think these are yours.'

As he handed her the box she could see that he was trying not to laugh.

'Max . . . I'm the one who should be sorry. All I can say by way of explanation is that I think I've had too much wine and I certainly didn't mean to fire a box of condoms at your head.'

He shrugged and picked up his wine glass. 'I've had worse things aimed at me. Don't worry about it.'

Joanne took a gulp of wine then another, wondering if she should call an end to the date but then she looked up at Max and he was smiling. He started to laugh and she joined in and soon, they were both laughing hard, tears rolling down their cheeks.

When they managed to compose themselves, Max reached across the table and took Joanne's hand. 'Thank you.'

'What for?'

'I haven't laughed that much in ages. I've had such a good evening.'

'Me too.'

Her face was aching, she felt sweaty from laughing and she was more embarrassed than she'd been in years. But she'd also managed to forget about her troubles and to enjoy the evening with this lovely man.

'Can I . . . Would it be okay if I walked you home?' Max asked.

'I'd really like that.'

'Me too.'

If they could laugh together, even in what could have been the most humiliating of moments, then it had to be a good sign. A very good sign indeed.

8

The next week passed with Joanne working at the café, thinking about how much she'd enjoyed her date with Max and watching the bids on her eBay items rise. As each one reached its conclusion, she found herself punching the air. She'd never get exactly what she paid back but at least she'd get something and all of it would help to reduce her debts, which in turn would take her closer to her future.

On Wednesday evening after work, she wrapped the sold items in brown paper, labelled them all then stuffed them into large bags. She'd pop to the village post office in the morning before her shift started and get them sent off. As she carried the bags downstairs to the hallway, her phone buzzed in her pocket. She wondered if it would be Max. She hadn't seen him since the Tuesday following their date and then it had only been brief when he'd come into the café to get a take-away coffee. It had been lovely to see him and her stomach had fluttered when he'd smiled at her then gently brushed her hand with his fingers as she handed him the coffee. They had sent texts following their date but they were friendly and jokey, avoiding discussing the condoms or almost kiss.

Joanne had played that scene over and over in her head since Friday, unable to stop imagining what it would have been like to kiss him. She worried that she was getting a bit carried away, that perhaps he hadn't wanted to kiss her and perhaps it would never happen, but at the same time it was pleasant to indulge in the sweet fantasy that kissing him would happen and that it would be wonderful.

She checked her phone but it was just a text from the bank reminding her to check her online statement, so she deleted the text and slid the phone back in her pocket, swallowing the disappointment that it wasn't Max.

'Gosh, Joanne, what a lot of bags!' Her mum stood in the hallway behind her, hands on hips, her cheeks rosy from a walk in the chilly evening air. Her parents often went on a walk after dinner, believing that it helped them to digest their food and avoid late night heartburn. They usually went to bed by 9 p.m., something that Joanne could empathise with because she was frequently exhausted after her shifts, but also something she was glad of when she wanted the TV to herself.

'It's things I've sold on eBay.'

'On eBay? That's nice, Joanne.'

'I've got to take them to the post office tomorrow. It's cleared out a lot of space in the spare room.'

'Wonderful!' Her mum nodded. 'When you've sold it all, I can set that back up as an ironing and sewing room.'

Guilt settled on Joanne's shoulders like a lead weight. Her spending habits had meant that she'd taken up the spare room with her purchases when her mum and dad could have used it for other purposes, as well as the shed. She had been selfish and vowed to be more thoughtful from here on as well as more frugal.

'That will be lovely, Mum. You can start making patchwork quilts again, can't you?'

'I can and I have some other ideas too. I've seen some lovely patterns since I discovered Etsy.'

Joanne felt a rush of love for her mum so she stepped towards her and hugged her tight.

'Ohh! What's that for?' Her mum chuckled.

'Because I love you.'

'I love you too.'

'Right,' Joanne released her mum then stretched her arms above her head, feeling her spine clicking in ways she was quite sure it shouldn't be. 'I'm going to run a bubble bath and have a soak.'

'Good idea.' Her mum smiled. 'I'm going to put the kettle on.'

Joanne padded up the stairs and into the bathroom. She turned the taps on and poured some of her mum's magnolia bubble bath under the running water. While the bath filled, she went to her room and changed into her dressing gown then scooped her hair up and pinned it in a bun on top of her head. She was about to return to the bathroom when there was a furious pounding on the front door, so she rushed to the landing and peered down the stairs.

'Who is it, Rex?' Her mum followed her dad through the hall-way, a hand on his shoulder as if to hold him back from certain danger.

'I've no idea, Hilda.' He shook his head. 'I forgot my X-ray specs and can't see through the door.'

'There's no need to be facetious, Rex.'

'Be careful!' Joanne shouted from the landing. 'It could be anyone.'

Her dad turned and gave her a funny look that suggested she was stating the obvious, then went and opened the door.

Kerry burst into the hallway with the cold night air and threw herself into her dad's arms.

'Dad!' she cried. He staggered backwards under the impact of Kerry's embrace. When he found his balance, he held his eldest daughter away from him so he could look at her.

'Kerry? What is it, love?' he asked then he peered over Kerry's head and out of the door. 'Oh! Quick, come on in children,' he said. 'It's freezing out there.'

Lottie and Henry came through the front door, teeth chatter-ing, faces pale.

'What a lovely surprise.' Joanne's mum hugged the children then ushered them through to the kitchen, but from the top of the stairs Joanne saw the concern on her face. 'I bet you'd like a hot chocolate.'

'I'll be down now; I'll just turn the taps off,' Joanne called out although she wasn't sure if anyone heard her.

She returned to the bathroom just in time to stop the bath overflowing and took a minute to digest what had just happened. Kerry never arrived unannounced; never ever. She was organised, liked her weeknights at home to ensure she was prepared for the following day at school. Even a phone call that hadn't been planned could send her into frenzy of anxiety and set her ranting about how inconsiderate others could be. So, for her to turn up like that, something must be wrong. They might not be close anymore, but Joanne would never want Kerry to be upset. She loved her far too much for that.

She hurried downstairs to the kitchen where her mum was squirting cream on the top of two steaming mugs of hot chocolate. 'Lottie, would you like to get the marshmallows too?'

'Yes please, Nanny.' The little girl went to the cupboard next to the fridge and took out a bag that had been clipped with a peg.

'You sprinkle some on for you and Henry and I'll be back in a moment. I just need to ask your Aunty Joanne something.'

'Aunty Jo!' The children ran to her, drinks temporarily forgotten, and hugged her tight. She pressed kisses to their heads, noticing that they both smelt of school and something fried, which was very unusual for them. Even when they were with childminders, Kerry always had them put on clean clothes after school, fed them a healthy dinner when they got home and ensure they bathed early evening, but it seemed that today had been different.

'Hello sweethearts. Lovely to see you on a Thursday,' she said, smiling, hoping that her smile covered her growing confusion.

'Yes, Mummy said we just had to come and see you all. She said she couldn't stay another minute in *that* house with *that* man.' Lottie twisted her mouth awkwardly as if realising that she shouldn't have repeated what her mum had said.

Joanne glanced over Lottie's head and saw her own alarm reflected in her mum's expression.

What on earth had happened?

'Why don't you have your hot chocolates while Nanny and I have a quick chat then one of us can make you a snack?' Joanne gently nudged the children towards the table.

They sat down and Lottie opened the bag and started dropping marshmallows over the cream that was quickly melting.

'Aunty Jo?' Henry flicked his head to get his fringe out of his eyes. With his pale skin and smattering of freckles, he was simply adorable and Joanne wanted to scoop him up and cuddle him.

'Yes, angel?'

'My daddy wath crying. He told me before that big boyth don't cry when I feld over in the park and . . . but . . . he wath crying.' Her urge to hug him tight grew.

'Oh dear.' Joanne wrung her hands together. 'I'm sure he's all right. I'll ring him and check for you in a bit, okay?'

Henry nodded and his ginger hair flopped over his forehead again.

'Mum?' She nodded at the hallway and when her mum had joined her out there, she pulled the door behind them, leaving it open a crack in case the children needed her. 'Any idea what's going on?'

'None at all. But those poor little darlings.' Her mum's eyes glistened. 'And Kerry . . . I've never seen her like that before.'

'Nor me. It's very strange.'

'Why don't you go and find out what's happening, and I'll make the children some supper. Just in case they haven't had much this evening.'

Joanne entered the lounge slowly, her hands raised as if entering a hostile situation. 'Only me!'

Her dad and Kerry were sitting on the sofa in front of the window. Kerry looked up at her and sniffed then buried her face in her hands again.

'Uh . . . can I help at all?' Joanne asked.

Her dad grimaced as she sat on the chair and shrugged. He was clearly at a loss too.

'It's just . . . he's just . . . such a pig.' Kerry mumbled into her hands, her shoulders shaking as she sobbed. 'A . . . bloody . . . bloody arrogant pig!'

Joanne felt her eyes widen. She couldn't recall hearing Kerry swear since they were teenagers, so this was even more shocking. Her dad's face showed that he was thinking the same thing and as he gently patted Kerry's back, Joanne realised that he was really struggling. He was such a lovely man but he never knew what to do when one of the women in his life was this upset.

'Dad?' Joanne stood up. 'Why don't you go and help Mum with the children's supper and I'll stay here with Kerry?'

'Sure . . . good idea.' He nodded and stood up, relief etched on his features. As he passed her, he mouthed, 'Thank you.'

Joanne sat on the sofa next to Kerry and placed her hands in her lap.

'Kerry? Would you like to talk about what's happened?'

Kerry shook her head.

'Are you sure? See . . . Mum and Dad are very worried, as am I, and we can't help if we don't know why you're so upset.'

Kerry sniffed loudly. 'It's too embarrassing.'

'Oh . . . okay. Well, uh . . . Perhaps you could just tell me what the children think is going on and what your plans are for this evening. Do the children have school tomorrow?'

'No.' Kerry raised her head and Joanne fought the urge to recoil. Her sister looked terrible: her hair was damp with sweat and tears, clinging to her cheeks and forehead like seaweed, and her eyes were red and swollen. Joanne had never seen Kerry in such a mess. 'They have a teacher training day tomorrow so they don't have to go in. Jeremy was meant to have them as I have a big meeting with senior staff but . . . but . . . he said he can't have them now as he has a meeting he can't get out of. I asked him what I'm supposed to do and he said . . . he said . . . ' She sneezed and snot flew out of her nose and across the sofa between them. Joanne grabbed a tissue from the box on the table and handed it to

Kerry then used another one to wipe the sofa. Kerry seemed oblivious to what she'd just done and Joanne tried not to pull a face as she cleaned the snot away. She didn't mind wiping her niece and nephew's noses but this was taking it a bit far.

'What did he say?' Joanne asked, tossing the dirty tissue into the small wicker basket at the side of the sofa.

'That if I'm so good at doing it all, then surely I can sort out childcare for a day.'

Joanne gasped. She couldn't believe her brother-in-law would be so thoughtless or that he and Kerry would be at odds with each other. Jeremy and Kerry were always so together. They seemed to be in total agreement on just about everything. When Kerry had been pregnant, Joanne had been amazed when Kerry had bragged about how Jeremy massaged her feet and rubbed cream into her stretch marks. They had agreed on first names, middle names and the schools they wanted the children to attend before they were even born. They had it together in ways that Joanne could never imagine. She had thought that if she'd ever been a mum, she'd have been a bit slapdash, a bit last-minute, disorganised, not at all a pushy parent, probably more of a pushover. Couples like Jeremy and Kerry didn't argue over things like this, did they? They agreed on everything, from shampoo to university funds, from politics to music.

Or perhaps they didn't. Obviously, they didn't. Or Kerry wouldn't be sitting here sobbing. And she was sobbing again so Joanne rubbed her back gently. Then something occurred to her. Kerry had said that Jeremy commented on her being 'so good at doing it all'.

'Kerry . . . why did he say that? About you doing it all?'

'He . . . I . . . I've seen a job I'd like to go for but it's not local.'

'Oh . . . where is it?'

'Bristol.'

'Right.' Joanne did a quick calculation. It would be about two hours away by car, longer by train. 'That's quite a commute.'

Joanne nodded then pushed her hair back from her face and wiped her nose again. 'But it's a good job, a wonderful opportunity. It's what I've been working towards all my career.'

'Is it a headship?'

'Deputy head. The next step up from where I am now.'

'It sounds amazing.'

Kerry nodded and her face relaxed a bit. 'It's a good school with a new head and she's looking for someone to come in as deputy. I rang her last week and we had a chat and she said she liked what I had to say and told me to apply.'

'That sounds very positive.'

'It is. I know it's not a guarantee I'd get the job and the closing date isn't until the Friday after half-term but it's something to be positive about. I like the school where I am but there are too many of us keen to climb to the next level. You know how much my career has meant to me.'

'And there's nothing wrong with that at all.' Joanne nodded. 'You have every right to pursue a career.'

'Yes, I do. But . . . Jeremy . . . he's been so supportive ever since we met. But now . . . I don't know why but he's not so keen.'

'Because of the commute?'

'I suggested moving if I was successful with my application, and the post doesn't start until after Easter, so we'd have time to prepare, but he didn't like that idea, so I said I'd commute and he went quiet. This was last weekend after I'd spoken to the head teacher of the school, when I tried to have a conversation about it with him. I'd floated the idea before that but we hadn't had time to discuss it properly because we'd both been so busy. I put the children to bed then opened a bottle of wine and made a nice meal but when I broached the subject, he just snapped. He said I'd had it all my own way for years and that he couldn't take any more. I was shocked and went to bed in tears, but he didn't come after me, so I thought he needed time to cool down. Every time I tried to raise the subject this week, he's walked away, probably because he doesn't want to argue but then this evening he just erupted like a volcano. I don't know what to do, Joanne, I really don't. I guess I just can't go for it.'

Joanne mulled it over. This was a difficult situation for her sister.

'Kerry . . . What is it that he doesn't like about the idea?'

'Me being away from home for even longer. And it would be longer if I commute because it's two hours there and back by car. If I had parents' evenings and meetings, I wouldn't be home until after the children have gone to bed and it's likely I'd need to leave before they get up.' Her face had gone ashen and her eyes looked so sad that Joanne reached out to her and took her hand. Kerry stiffened for a moment but then she slowly relaxed and offered a small smile of gratitude.

'Only you and Jeremy can decide what to do.' Joanne met her sister's eyes and smiled. 'But I'm sure you'll do what's best.'

Kerry shook her head. 'I don't know what is for the best though. I want this job but even I can see that it will be difficult with the children being so young. If it had come along in ten years, even five, then they'd be a bit older and more able to understand. I worry about what I'm missing out on as it is with the hours I work right now. This new job would mean being away from them for longer and I know that I could turn around and find that they've turned into teenagers without me noticing. And I want to do what's best for them, Joanne, I really do.'

'I know you do.' Joanne patted Kerry's hand, nodding in what she hoped was a reassuring way.

'This job would mean a significant pay rise and I'd be even closer to running a school of my own but if I go for it and get it, I could lose my husband and my family.'

'I'm sure it won't come to that.' Joanne shook her head. 'Jeremy hasn't said as much has he?'

'He hasn't given me an ultimatum, but he's really annoyed with me. I don't like it at all. We're usually in agreement about things and yet it seems that I've managed to make him feel that he doesn't matter as much to me as he used to do and that the children aren't as important as my career.' She sank back on the cushions and closed her eyes. 'This is so difficult, Joanne. If he'd only consider moving then it wouldn't be such a dilemma.'

'What about his job?'

Kerry opened her eyes. 'He's so good at it that he'd have no problem finding another. He could even go freelance and get lots of high-paid work from private clients. He has plenty of contacts.'

Joanne knew Kerry was right. Jeremy had been successful and had an excellent reputation. He could even set up a new branch of the firm he was a partner in.

'Are you going to stay here tonight?' she asked.

'If that's okay? Will Mum and Dad mind?'

'Of course, they won't. It will be lovely to have you here. And isn't it half-term next week?'

Kerry nodded. 'I have to go to my meeting tomorrow but perhaps Mum and Dad will watch the children.'

'I'm sure they will. I only have a short shift at the café too, so I'll be around.'

'Is there room for us here though? Isn't the spare room full of your. . . things?'

'Didn't you see the bags in the hallway as you came in?'

'I was too busy sobbing.' Kerry snorted. 'It's not funny but even I can see how ridiculous it was to turn up like that. Dad looked like he'd pooped his pants.'

'Poor Dad. You did give him a scare. But everyone gets upset at some point and you are a human being, however much you like to come across as some kind of superhero. As for the bags, they're filled with things from upstairs and the shed. Not all of them, as I'm listing them online in waves, so I don't have too many things to watch at once, but everything that's left is in the shed, therefore the bedroom is now available.'

'My old room.' Kerry smiled and Joanne realised that even her strong older sister wanted to know that she could come home when she needed her family.

'Exactly. You can sleep there and the children can have my room.'

'Where will you sleep?'

'The sofa's fine.'

'Thank you, Joanne.' Kerry squeezed her hand tight. 'You're a good sister.'

'And you're a good wife and mum, but also an individual with a right to a career. It's just about finding balance.'

'How did you get so wise?'

'I have no idea because when it comes to my own life, I'm an absolute train wreck.'

'I guess it will do Jeremy good to have a few nights to himself anyway. Let him miss me and the children. I don't suppose there's any wine here is there? I could murder a glass.'

'I'll go and check.'

'Thanks again, little sister.'

'No problem.'

As Joanne went out into the hallway, she thought about what her sister had told her. She didn't envy Kerry having to make such a difficult decision, but she did feel sure that Kerry would make the right one for her family and for herself. She just hoped Jeremy would be as supportive as Kerry needed him to be, as supportive as she knew her sister had always been towards her husband.

9

The next morning, Kerry had set off early for work while Joanne had taken the bags of parcels to the post office then worked her shift at the café. She went home after the lunchtime rush to find her mum in the kitchen alone.

'Where is everyone?' she asked as she removed her coat and hung it over the back of a chair.

'Your dad has taken the children to the park for an hour. We thought the fresh air would do them good.' Her mum sat opposite her.

'That's nice. Didn't you want to go?'

'I had a few things to sort here, especially seeing as how it looks like Kerry will be staying a bit longer.'

'Is she?'

Her mum nodded. 'She sent a text earlier asking if it would be okay.'

'It'll be nice to have the children here, won't it?'

'Yes, dear.' Her mum placed her hands on the table, one cradling the other.

'Are you all right?' Joanne asked.

'I'm fine, Joanne. A bit worried about Kerry, Lottie and Henry, but I'm sure it will all come out in the wash.'

'I hope so.' Joanne pushed her shoulders back, aware that her night on the sofa had left her feeling stiff.

'Speaking of the wash . . . ' Her mum wrung her hands together. 'I was checking pockets as I always do, because you know how your dad tends to leave tissues in his and sometimes you leave tips from the café in yours and . . . well . . . when I stuck my hand in yours I found lots of bits of plastic.'

'Bits of plastic?' Joanne frowned as she tried to think what it could have been. Then it hit her. *The credit cards!*

'Yes. They were quite sharp and I cut my finger on one.' Her mum held up her left hand and Joanne saw the plaster on her forefinger.

'Ouch! I'm sorry about that. I forgot they were in there.'

'I emptied them onto the table and asked your dad what he thought they were then we realised that they were bank cards.'

Joanne swallowed; her mouth suddenly dry.

'Oh . . . ' She dragged a breath through gritted teeth.

'Is there something you'd like to tell me, Joanne?'

Joanne tried to swallow again but her mouth was as dry as a desert, so she found herself gagging instead.

'Joanne?' Her mum reached across the table. 'What is it?'

She reached up to her throat and rubbed it but she really couldn't swallow.

'Do you need some water?'

She nodded and her mum hurried to the sink and filled a glass then handed it to her.

'Here. Drink this quickly.'

She gulped the water down then swilled some around her mouth.

'That's better, thanks.'

Her mum sat back down and folded her hands together on the table. Joanne realised that she was going to have to be honest, even though this was the one thing she had hoped to avoid for as long as possible.

'Mum . . . '

'Yes, dear.'

'I do need to tell you something but I don't want you to worry.'

Her mum bobbed her head then straightened her back as if bracing herself.

'They were credit cards. I cut them up the other day when Roxie and Lila were here and I shoved them into my pocket so you wouldn't see them . . . then I forgot all about them.'

'Go on.'

'You know all the things that I'm selling and aiming to sell.'

'Yes.'

Joanne cleared her throat.

'Well . . . I didn't actually win them.'

'No?' Her mum's eyebrows wavered on her forehead like two uncertain furry caterpillars.

'No. See . . . I bought them. With credit cards.'

She held her breath and watched her mum's face, her heart sinking as myriad emotions danced across it. Surely her mum must be horrified and disappointed at her behaviour? She was in debt and it was all her own fault.

'Are you in debt, Joanne?'

She nodded, a lump forming in her throat.

'Is it bad?'

She nodded again.

'How bad is it?'

Joanne coughed to clear her throat. 'I'm trying to sort it out. Roxie and Lila have been helping me—'

'You're not taking money from your friends?' Her mum's expression had turned to one that wouldn't have been amiss in a horror movie.

'Goodness, no!'

'Thank heaven for that. So how are they helping?'

'They encouraged me to cut up the cards and to list the things on eBay to sell them so I could start to pay back the debts.

Roxie in particular has been very helpful and because of her I can finally see a way through.'

'Joanne?'

'Yes?'

'Why didn't you tell me and your dad about this? We could have helped.'

Joanne exhaled slowly and laced her fingers together in her lap then started to pick at a cuticle as anxiety swirled inside her.

'I was so ashamed, Mum. It started as just one card then I saw something about a balance transfer so I did that but I didn't get rid of the first card and before I knew it, I had maxed both of them out. I got another card to transfer the balances and it just kept going until I was paying one off with the other then swapping the following month. Then I ended up using my overdraft facility and . . . well . . . It spiralled out of control.'

'Oh, Joanne.' Her mum shook her head. 'We could have helped you before it got this bad. How much are we talking about?'

Joanne hung her head. 'I don't like to say.'

'Do you want to write it down?'

'Like in a movie?'

'In a movie?'

'When they're negotiating a deal and they don't want to say the figure out loud?'

'If you like.' Her mum shrugged then pushed a notepad across the table. The first page of it had the weekly shopping list on it so Joanne flipped it over then slowly wrote the amount she owed. Written down, it didn't look quite as bad as it sounded in her head, but she still didn't want to show her mum.

'It won't be that bad in a week because of the items I've already sold. I'll pay it off as soon as I get all the money through from the first lot of sales.'

Her mum reached out for the pad but Joanne couldn't seem to let go of it.

'Let me see, Joanne.'

She made a conscious effort to peel her fingers away from the paper then pushed it towards her mum.

'Hmmm. It could be worse.'

'Really?'

'Yes.' Her mum tore the paper from the pad then crumpled it up. 'And we can help you with this.'

'But how?'

'Your dad and I have been saving for you and Kerry ever since you were born. We didn't have a lot back then but we put away what we could. Kerry had her money when she got married to help pay for everything. We were waiting to do the same for you.'

'Until I got married?'

'Yes.'

Joanne buried her head in her hands. 'I'm a huge disappointment, aren't I? Not only have I got myself into debt, failed to find a career or even to move out but I've also not managed to fall in love and settle down.'

'You are not a disappointment, Joanne.'

'But you and Dad . . . you're so proud of Kerry. She's got a great job, a devoted husband . . . most of the time anyway . . . and she's given you two gorgeous grandchildren. She's been no trouble at all, has only ever made you smile. What have I ever done to make you proud?'

'Firstly, Kerry has had her own troubles, so she's not been as perfect as you might think.'

'Like what?'

'That's something I'm not about to disclose. Just as I would keep anything you told me secret, unless you said it was all right to share it. Anyway, back to my points . . . Secondly, your dad and I have been very proud of you for many reasons. You're a wonderful daughter, a kind and caring person. You're lovely inside and out and our pride in you is not based on whether you find a man, or woman, to marry. We love you unconditionally, Joanne, and I thought that was something you knew.'

Joanne swallowed hard. Her mum was right. Joanne had always felt loved and supported. Her parents had never criticised how she lived her life or belittled her in any way. They had celebrated her GCSE results even though they'd been far lower than Kerry's. They had made a fuss of her on all her birthdays and supported her decision to go travelling straight after leaving college following the first year of her A levels. She'd known that they'd been anxious about it, but they had trusted her, even when she was barely eighteen, to do what she thought was right with her life. When she'd come home, rather disillusioned with her attempt at a bohemian lifestyle, they hadn't said 'We told you so . . .' or mocked her in any way. They'd welcomed her back and accepted that she was taking her time to find the career she wanted. Even when her thirtieth birthday came and went and the spare bedroom and shed were filled with Joanne's purchases, when she showed no sign of moving out as the years passed by, they didn't put pressure on her to move out or to find a job that paid more than working at the café did. They had only ever been loving and supportive and she knew how incredibly lucky she was to have them. Too lucky probably because not many parents would have been so understanding, so kind, so accepting.

'I do know, Mum. You and Dad are amazing, and I don't ever want you to feel I've taken you both for granted.'

'We don't, love. You're an individual and you're different from Kerry. We have never compared you both. We love you just as you are.'

'I'm so grateful, Mum, but I also know that it's time to pull myself together and to stand on my own feet.'

'Well . . . if you let me and your dad help you a bit with your finances, then you will be able to get on your feet faster than you would otherwise.'

'I can't let you do that. You've done enough for me.'

'The money is yours, Joanne. We put it away for you. Kerry had hers and this is yours.'

'I don't know what to say.'

'Just say yes.'

Joanne nodded slowly, wondering exactly how much money her mum was talking about.

'Here.' Her mum had just written something on the notepad and she pushed it across the table to Joanne.

Joanne gasped. 'How is there so much?'

'We had a little lottery win. Not enough to pack up and move to Florida but enough to put away a bit more for you and Kerry. It topped up what we'd already saved.'

'But why didn't you and Dad have a few holidays or buy a bigger house?'

'Why would we want to do that? We had everything we needed right here and all we've ever wanted was to give you and Kerry the best we could.'

Joanne's vision blurred and she wiped at her eyes. Her hands came away wet.

'This is too much, Mum. I don't need it all.'

'After you've paid off what you can from selling some of the things on eBay, you can put what you need towards your debts then use the rest as a deposit on a place of your own. If you want, that is. There's no need for you to move out, and we do love having you here, but if you feel you'd like some independence now . . . then you have that option. As I said, we were waiting to see if you fell in love and then we'd have paid the money towards your wedding as a big surprise, but seeing as how your need is more immediate . . . It makes sense for you to use the money now.'

'Thank you so much. I'm so grateful.'

Her mum shook her head and waved a hand as if she hadn't just given Joanne a gift that would make all of her problems go away. The thought that she could even consider looking for a place of her own was so exciting. It wasn't that she didn't like living with her parents because they were so easy-going and she loved them dearly but having some space and knowing that they would be getting some time alone together, which they certainly deserved, would make her feel better too.

Life could begin a whole lot faster than she'd anticipated and it was all thanks to her wonderful parents and dearest friends.

10

'What about this one, Aunty Jo?' Lottie held up a costume and Joanne looked at it then turned to Kerry.

'What do you think, Kerry?'

Her sister smiled. 'If that's what Lottie wants then she should have it.'

Joanne gazed at the costume. It wasn't what she had thought Lottie might go for, as the previous year her niece had been insistent that she would grow up to be a mermaid. However, it seemed that her ambitions had changed and the costume she had chosen this year was that of a werewolf.

'What about you, Henry?'

'I don't know. I'm not thure.' His bottom lip protruded, and he seemed bewildered. 'There'th tho many.'

Joanne wrapped an arm around his shoulders. 'Tell you what, why don't we choose one together?'

He nodded and leant against her, clearly glad to have some support.

Joanne looked over at Lottie who was now perusing the array of colourful wigs, then at Kerry. Her sister had suggested the shopping trip to the large shopping centre — a large, sprawling rectangle built on the site of a former football stadium — that was twenty-five minutes from the village the previous day. Roxie had dropped by to speak to Joanne and had invited Kerry and the children to her Halloween party then and there, something that Joanne had been grateful for because since her arrival, Kerry had seemed very low indeed. Right now, Kerry was staring hard at her phone, seeming oblivious to her children and surroundings. Joanne wondered if she'd received a text from Jeremy or if it was something to do with the job she wanted to apply for.

What Joanne did know was that she wanted Henry to feel safe and secure and not daunted by the many costumes on offer, so she took his hand and led him towards a different rail.

'How about being a pumpkin, Henry?'

She pulled out a hanger with a bright orange costume on it and lowered it to his level.

'A punkin?' He touched the costume. 'Like a big ball.'

'Yes. Like an orange ball.'

He smiled. 'Will you be a punkin too?'

'I guess I could take a look around and see if there's something that will fit me.'

'Yeth!' He tugged at her hand and pulled her across the shop.

Half an hour later, they had paid and left the shop with their purchases.

They made their way to a café at the far end of the shopping centre that had an outdoor space where children could play. While Joanne ordered frothy lattes for her and Kerry, Lottie and Henry ran off to the swings.

'There you go.' Joanne set the tall glass mugs on the table along with drinks for the children then sat opposite her sister on the wooden picnic bench. It was sunny but the wind was cold so she wrapped her hands around the glass mug and hunched forwards, tugging her scarf up higher around her neck and her woolly beret down lower over her ears.

They sat quietly for a while, watching the children play with small twin boys they'd met on the helter-skelter slide. Their energy and enthusiasm for climbing the steps to the top of the slide was admirable, especially seeing as how the reward seemed to be over so quickly. But they did it again and again, undaunted.

Joanne let her gaze wander from the children to Kerry. She was sitting with her legs crossed, arms wrapped around her body as she watched her children. Her eyes were hidden by oversized designer sunglasses but her skin was pale and seemed to be stretched over her cheekbones. She'd seemed distracted as they'd wandered around the fancy dress shop and Joanne had been able to sense her sadness, hanging like mist in the air and now she seemed even more lost.

'Kerry?' She reached out and touched Kerry's hand and her sister jumped as if she'd been fast asleep.

'Hmm?'

'You okay?'

The question was ridiculous in light of what Kerry was dealing with right now but Joanne didn't know what else to say.

'Hmm.' Kerry nodded.

'Do you want to talk about it?'

Kerry removed her sunglasses revealing dark purple shadows and bloodshot eyes.

'I wish I knew where to start.'

'Have you managed to speak to Jeremy?'

Kerry nodded. 'Briefly. Every day we try to find a way through but it's so difficult. I want to do what's best for my family but I know that if I'm not happy in my career then it will impact upon family life too.'

'Of course it will. You have to think of yourself as well.'

'Oh, you don't understand.' Kerry frowned then rubbed at her eyes. When she lowered her hands the skin around her eyes was red and blotchy.

'I'm trying.' Joanne sipped her coffee.

'I know . . . but you've never been in a long-term relationship, never had children, hell you've never even had a career!'

Joanne put her drink down and laced her fingers together, trying not to let her sister's sharp words sting. Just then, Lottie came running over, cheeks pink, eyes bright, and her hat leaning precariously to one side on top of her hair.

'Is that my drink?' She pointed at the bottle of juice.

'Yes there's one for you and one for Henry.'

'Thank you, Aunty Jo.' Lottie accepted the bottle and took a long drink. 'Yummy. Now I'm going back on the slide.'

'Be careful!' Joanne and Kerry said simultaneously.

As Lottie ran off they looked at each other and laughed. The last thing Joanne wanted to do was to argue with Kerry. Her sister was prickly at the moment but she was suffering so her angst wasn't at all surprising.

'Oh Joanne, I'm so sorry.' Kerry shook her head. 'I'm such a cow.'

'No you're not.'

'I am and don't try to make me feel better. There's no excuse for attacking you and your life choices just because I'm miserable. I mean . . . look at you. You're happy right? You're so laid-back. You have your café job, you live at home so you have no financial worries and you're strong and independent so you don't feel the need to have a partner.'

'Well . . . things might not be as they seem, you know.'

Kerry's eyes widened. 'No?'

'Look . . . for one, I do like my job at the café but it doesn't mean I haven't considered other career options. It's more that nothing has ever jumped out at me. Two, I live at home because I don't have a choice. I am in debt up to my eyeballs and then some. And three, you're right about the whole partner thing because, no, I don't need one but sometimes it would be nice to have a companion.'

Kerry's stared at her unblinking.

'You're in debt?'

'Where do you think all those things came from?'

'The clothes and shoes and everything else at Mum and Dad's?'

'Yes. I . . . I maxed out credit cards to buy them. I got myself into a right mess but finally. . . I'm sorting it out.'

'That's good to hear because financial trouble can be awful.'

'It is, believe me.'

'But even hearing that . . . you need to know that I always admired you. You seem to have it so together. Don't get me wrong, I love my husband and children but I have found myself envying your freedom to do whatever you want, to go wherever you want, to sleep through the night without a care in the world.'

'You envied me?' Joanne's voice rose in surprise.

'Yes, of course.'

'I thought you always disapproved of me.'

'Goodness, no. Not at all. You're amazing.'

'But you and Jeremy always seemed to look down your noses at me.'

'Did we?'

'I thought so . . . sometimes.'

'If we did that, Joanne, then I am so sorry. It might have happened from time to time but I suspect that what you took for disapproval was probably more like envy. You always seemed so close to Mum and Dad and I sometimes felt like an outsider.'

'We've both got things wrong, haven't we?'

'Kind of a grass is greener scenario, I guess.'

'So it would seem.'

They finished their coffees, letting what they'd shared sink in.

'About me and Jeremy.' Kerry cleared her throat. 'I want to find a way through this. . . to try to fix my marriage. I love him, I really do, but we're both going to need to compromise.'

'Isn't that what marriage is about?' Joanne smiled.

'It really is. I'm going to take this week to spend some time with the children and with you, Mum and Dad then I'll ask him to meet with me next weekend. That way, we can both have some space over half-term then try to find a way forwards before I go back to school. I need to make a decision anyway because this is a time sensitive issue.'

'I'm sure you can work it out. You have too much to lose and you've been together for such a long time.'

Kerry nodded, her features relaxing now that she'd made a decision, and Joanne was filled with warmth that she was able to share a moment like this with her sister. Kerry was letting her guard down, reaching out to her family and it meant that Joanne could be the sister that she'd always wanted to be.

11

The day of the Halloween party had arrived. Joanne already had a headache and it wasn't because of her late shift at the café the previous day. Lottie and Henry had been awake since 6 a.m. and they'd made their way downstairs where they'd bounced around on the sofa to share their excitement about their costumes with Joanne. She'd been fast asleep, dreaming about being in a car with Max as they drove along an American freeway, the wind in their hair, the sun warming their skin. They'd been laughing, though about what she wasn't sure now as the dream drifted away.

'Are you excited, Aunty Jo?' Lottie asked as she snuggled under the duvet and stroked Joanne's hair.

'Uh . . . I guess so.' Joanne yawned, longing to close her eyes and sink back into sleep.

'Mummy's not. She's still asleep.' Lottie pulled a face. 'We tried to wake her already.'

'She'th thnoring.' Henry shook his head.

'Mummy's just tired, guys.' Joanne opened her arms and the children squeezed closer to her. She kissed their heads, enjoying their baby scent, then something else caught her nostrils and she looked down at Henry.

'Henry what are you wearing?'

Colour flooded his cheeks.

'It's my nightie,' Lottie said matter-of-factly.

'It's very nice but didn't you go to bed in tiger pyjamas?' Joanne tried to think back to what he'd been wearing when she'd got home from the café and he was standing at the top of the stairs rubbing his eyes. She'd gone up, taken him back to bed and tucked him in, gently kissing his forehead.

'He did but . . . promise you won't tell?' Lottie gazed up at her, eyes wide and hand held up with the little finger wiggling. 'Pinky promise.'

'Of course. Pinky promise.' Joanne nodded and eased her arm out from behind her niece then curled her little finger around Lottie's.

'Henry had a wet night.'

'Oh . . . ' Joanne turned back to Henry and her heart almost broke at the devastation on his face. 'Well that's okay.'

'I don't like it,' Henry whispered. 'I'm not a baby. I'm dry at night.'

'He has been dry for ages, Aunty Jo but since we've been here . . . he's had a few . . . accidents.' Lottie spoke quietly, her eyes fixed on Joanne's face. 'It's not his fault. He just misses Daddy and home.'

'Of course he does. Of course you both do.'

Joanne hugged them tight, wishing she could restore their sense of security.

'Everyone has accidents, Henry, and no one needs to know about them.'

'Do you?' He gazed at her without blinking and she paused for a moment then knew what to say. 'Perhaps not in terms of having a wet night but I've had other types of accidents.'

'Like buying stuff you don't actually need?' Lottie asked, five going on fifty.

'That's right.' How Lottie knew about that she had no idea but then children often overheard things they shouldn't. 'So you gave Henry your nightie because his pyjamas were wet did you?'

'Yes.'

'Okay, well why don't you creep upstairs and get anything that's wet and bring it down. I'll pop it in the washer then make us some tea and toast.'

'Yes please!' Lottie jumped up. 'But can we have hot chocolate, please?'

'Of course you can.'

Joanne stood up and held out a hand for Henry and he took it then slid off the sofa to his feet. Joanne realised that he probably needed a bath too, but she didn't want to make a big deal about it so she'd get them some breakfast first then deal with getting him clean.

When he reached up to her she leant forwards and picked him up and he curled his arms around her neck. There was a faint odour of urine but mainly he smelt like a sleepy child and her heart filled with love for him and for Lottie. She would miss the children when they returned home and hoped that she'd get to see more of them. Of course, if they did move for Kerry's job then she might see even less of them and that would be awful, but her niece and nephew deserved security and happiness and she wanted to see them get that back more than anything in the world.

'Are we ready to go?' Joanne's mum stood in the kitchen and smiled at her family. 'I must say that I think we all look quite fabulous!'

Joanne nodded. Her mum and dad were dressed as zombies, Lottie was a werewolf, she and Henry were pumpkins and as for Kerry, she looked very sophisticated in a fitted black catsuit complete with cat ear headband holding back her ginger bob. She'd drawn whiskers on her cheeks and coloured the tip of her nose black.

'Let's take a selfie, shall we?' her dad asked, making Joanne giggle. He'd been taking selfies all week with Lottie's encouragement and Joanne had loved seeing him pout and pose alongside his granddaughter. They were making precious memories that Lottie would carry through her life.

They huddled together and he held the phone up high. 'Say Happy Halloween!'

'HAPPY HALLOWEEN!' they all sang as he clicked the button several times.

'Let's get our coats on and make our way to the party!' Her mum clapped her hands and they all headed out into the hallway where coats and shoes had been laid out ready, chosen to fit over their costumes.

Joanne found it a bit difficult to get her arms through her coat with her body being a big round pumpkin, but her dad helped her then he wrapped a thick scarf around her neck. Her head was already covered with an orange hood complete with pumpkin stalk and she had silky orange gloves on her hands that she suspected she'd have to remove afterwards because they were very slippery and would make holding a drink impossible. She'd already dropped her phone twice when checking it for texts from Max so had given up and stuffed it in the pocket of her costume. Max had said he might come if he could find a suitable costume and she really hoped he would do.

As she headed for the door, Henry grabbed her hand and they waddled out onto the street together. The evening was dark, the street lights casting a warm glow on the pavement, the sky beyond them velvety black with pinpricks of shimmering silver. The pavement crunched beneath their feet, frost already forming, and their breath emerged in front of them in great clouds that disappeared into the air. Joanne and Henry walked on ahead while her parents, niece and sister followed, Lottie chatting away about how a werewolf would beat a vampire in a fight, insisting that she'd seen it on TV.

'I'm tho ecthited.' Henry squeezed her hand.

'I know. Me too.' Joanne smiled.

'Will there be pritheth?'

'Pritheth?' Joanne frowned.

'For costumeth.' He skipped along and Joanne almost started to skip too as her arm was jogged up and down.

'I expect so. Roxie does like to make a big deal of Halloween and always puts on a great party.'

'I with my Daddy wath coming.'

Joanne's heart squeezed. 'I know, sweetheart. I know.'

Lottie danced up to them and took Henry's hand then said, 'Let's race the grown-ups.'

He giggled and they ran on ahead, Joanne resisting the urge to shout at them to be careful not to slip.

Kerry appeared at her side, her eyes wide with concern, and Joanne nodded. Her sister had overheard what Henry said.

'It will all be okay, Kerry,' Joanne said. 'Don't you worry.'

'I'm trying not to.'

Kerry slid her arm through Joanne's and they walked together, sisters joined by love, life, and understanding. They'd lost their closeness over the years but they were finding their way back.

Roxie's driveway was like a movie set. There were cobwebs draped over the hedges and trees, pumpkins in a range of sizes lining the driveway and front steps, and the front windows were decorated with tiny pumpkin fairy lights.

Joanne's niece and nephew gasped with delight at everything they saw. When they reached the front door they both screamed as a skeleton standing like a butler to the side of the door leant forwards and laughed loudly. It seemed to be activated by movement and Joanne wasn't looking forward to getting any closer to it.

The door swung open and a tiny pumpkin raced out and barked at them, making the children giggle.

'It's okay, it's Glenda.' Joanne crouched down and rubbed the dog's head but her movement set the skeleton off and Glenda started to growl at it.

'Come here, Glenda!' Roxie scooped the dog up in her arms. 'Sorry everyone, she's overexcited today and she bloody hates that skeleton. She pulled one of its feet off earlier and I think she's buried it in the back garden.'

Joanne looked down at the skeleton's legs and sure enough, it was missing a foot.

'I love her costume,' Joanne said.

'Isn't she the cutest?' Roxie kissed the dog's tiny nose. 'My pug-sized pumpkin.'

'You look amazing too.' Joanne gazed at her friend in awe. Roxie was wearing a Victorian style red gown with a lace overlay that did up at her throat and waist then flowed out from the long full skirt. Her face was made-up to resemble a skull and her black hair was swept up into a high bun and streaked with white. Her fingernails were painted black and black pointy shoes peeped out from under the dress.

'I'm a dead Victorian.' Roxie laughed then shrugged. 'I just liked the lace overlay and silky skirts. And you all look wonderful too.' She smiled at Lottie and Henry, at Joanne's parents and at Joanne. 'Come on in and have a drink. Some of the guests are here already and the bar is open!'

'Is Fletcher behind it?'

'Oh yes, darling, Fletcher is doing his best Tom Cruise impression.'

Joanne frowned.

'You know from the movie *Cocktail*? From the late eighties? No?'

Joanne shook her head.

'I remember that one. Loved Tom in that.' Joanne's mother clapped her hands. 'I had your father trying to shake me a cocktail for months afterwards but he just didn't do it quite like Tom.'

Joanne looked at her dad and he rolled his eyes.

'Your mum had a huge crush on him and watched that movie every day for a month, I swear. I had a repetitive strain injury from trying to make all the cocktails she wanted to try.' He winked and Joanne smiled in return.

'What's a repetitive strain injury, Grandad?' Lottie asked.

'I'll explain later.' He ushered the children inside and Joanne hung back with Roxie in the hallway.

'Everything okay with you now?' Roxie asked.

'Yes, much better.' Joanne nodded.

'I'm so glad to hear that. You look like a weight's been lifted.'

Joanne looked down at her rounded middle then patted the front of the pumpkin suit. 'Really?'

Roxie nudged her. 'You know what I mean.'

'I do. And yes, thanks to you and Lila, and to my mum and dad who have also been able to help out.'

'That's wonderful news. Now . . . shall we go and get a drink to celebrate your fresh start?'

'Brilliant idea.'

As they walked through the hallway, Roxie set Glenda down and the pug ran through to the large kitchen-diner.

'Your uh . . . friend has already arrived.'

'My friend?'

'Max.'

'Oh.' Joanne's stomach flipped over.

'He looks gorgeous. Some sort of sexy sparkling vampire, I think. Well . . . he does have glitter on his face and the backs of his hands and his hair is gelled up into a quiff, so I'm assuming that's the look he was going for.'

'Right.' Joanne glanced at the mirror in the hallway, ruing her decision to come as a pumpkin. If Max was a sexy vampire, what would he think of her bright orange rotundity?

'Don't go all insecure on me now. You look delightful and I love that you picked an outfit to match little Henry.'

'He wanted me to match him.'

'That's because he loves you.'

'You're right. He's adorable.'

'And so are you.'

Roxie gave her a nudge through the kitchen doorway and Joanne lifted her chin and smiled, determined to have a good time.

❧

At the bar set up in the garden marquee, Fletcher — who was dressed as Frankenstein's monster — mixed up some cocktails then added colourful straws with tiny paper skulls and spiders on the ends of them. Joanne accepted a glass filled with something green and glittery and Roxie explained that it was a poison apple cocktail. When she sipped it, she found it crisp and tart, and quite delicious.

'It's strong so don't drink it too quickly.' Roxie grinned. 'Or we'll have to roll you home.'

Joanne watched as the children ran off to play with others from the village, comparing costumes and shrieking with laughter at the array of Halloween foods on offer including spider biscuits, witches' fingers, eyeball jelly, kiwi slime pies, cheese pastry snakes and spooky spinach dip. Lottie and Henry seemed happy this evening and she was grateful for that, but as she looked around for Kerry, she couldn't see her and hoped she was all right.

After speaking to some of the villagers, she moved out of the way of people heading for the space set up as a dance floor and found a quiet corner where she could enjoy her drink and have a good look around. Music filled the marquee as the DJ set up on a small stage began his set and Joanne found herself swaying to the music, relaxing in the warm friendly atmosphere. Lila and Ethan, dressed as skeletons that glowed in the dark, came to talk to her for a while and she told them how impressed she was with their costumes that Lila had made.

After they'd headed to the dance floor, she became aware of someone standing behind her.

'Hello there.' The voice sent shivers of delight down her spine and she turned to find Max.

'Hi.' She was breathless at how sexy he looked with his hair gelled up at the front, his skin sparkling with glitter, his usually dark brown eyes a warm amber.

He smiled, revealing plastic fangs, and her heart rate increased.

'I know it's a bit cliched, but I did love the books and always fancied seeing myself as a vampire.'

'You look incredible.' Joanne swallowed hard. 'I loved those books too.'

'I love your outfit,' he said, his eyes roaming over her. 'Very cute.'

'My nephew wanted me to match him.'

'That's adorable.'

'Can I get you a drink?' he asked.

'Go on then.' Joanne handed him her empty glass and watched while he went to the bar and selected two glasses of something red. He returned to her side and handed her one.

'I thought we could try a blood orange transfusion.'

'Lovely.'

They clinked glasses then sipped the drink and Joanne felt the strong cocktail warming her insides and flooding into her bloodstream. Her eyes kept returning to Max, she felt unable to look away.

'I was wondering . . .' he said, leaning closer so she could hear him over the music. 'Have you ever been kissed by a vampire?'

She shook her head, glancing around, but people were dancing and engaged in conversation, milling around admiring costumes and enjoying the buffet.

'Would you like to try it?'

She nodded, unable to speak because her heart was racing.

He held her gaze, the amber of his contact lenses making his lashes seem thicker and darker than usual. He took a step closer to her then looked down and grinned because her big belly was in the way. When he removed his fangs, she felt like she would faint with anticipation.

The kiss when it came was gentle, his lips brushing hers like a butterfly's wings and she gasped.

'I've been wanting to do that since our date.' He took her hand. 'I thought I might have a better chance looking like this.'

'What? But why? You're so handsome.'

He laughed self-consciously. 'Thanks, and please don't tell anyone but I'm also incredibly shy and the costume gave me some confidence . . . as did the first cocktail Fletcher mixed for me.' He fanned his face. 'It was very strong.'

Joanne's attention was dragged from Max and over to the entrance to the marquee where she could see Fletcher holding up his hands and shaking his head.

'What's going on?' she asked but Max shrugged so she placed her glass on a table and hurried over, worried that someone had been hurt.

'Where's my wife?' It was Jeremy, at least it sounded like Jeremy but he looked like a wizard in a black cape and pointy hat with a fake nose glued to his face.

'He's my brother-in-law,' Joanne explained to Fletcher as she went to his side. 'Are you okay?'

He looked at her over the huge plastic nose and she saw that his eyes were glistening. 'I was on my way to a colleague's Halloween party but I found myself driving to the village instead. The children told me that they were coming here this evening and I . . . I need to see Kerry. Where is she?'

He peered around the marquee and Joanne followed his gaze, spotting her sister in the middle of the dance floor, standing alone, her long tail hooked over her arm, her eyes wide with shock.

'Kerry!' Jeremy shouted then hurried across the dance floor just as the music stopped, the DJ now aware of the scene unfolding. Lottie and Henry appeared behind Kerry, their eyes and mouths wide as they watched their parents. 'I love you so much and I've missed you desperately.'

Kerry seemed frozen, her face expressionless. Joanne was torn between wanting to rush to her side and by feeling the need to give her space.

Jeremy went down on his knees and took Kerry's hands. 'I love you and the children. You're my world and I can't live without you. All our married life you've worked incredibly hard, never complained, never shied away from the demands of family life. You are the bravest person I know, the strongest woman I have ever met and I adore you. I want you to go for the new job. You deserve it and the children and I will move with you. I'll look into setting up freelance in Bristol. Just say you still want me because I can't live without you. Please?'

Kerry was staring down at her husband as if she couldn't believe what she was hearing. The marquee fell silent. Joanne found herself holding her breath.

Then Kerry knelt and slid her arms around Jeremy. 'I love you too and I'm sorry for worrying you. We need to talk but we can find a way through this, I'm sure.'

They stood up, still holding each other, and Lottie and Henry rushed to them then the four of them hugged. The DJ took it as a sign to restart the music and 'Monster Mash' began to play. The dance floor soon filled up and Joanne felt herself sag with relief. It seemed that everything would work out for Kerry after all.

'Thank goodness for that.' Her mum and dad joined her, both smiling as they watched their daughter dancing with her husband and children.

'Indeed,' her dad said. 'Shall we dance, Hilda?'

'Don't mind if I do.'

While her parents strutted off and started to move on the dance floor, Joanne felt a hand on her arm.

'Dance with a vampire?' Max asked.

'I'd love to.'

He led her towards her parents and took her in his arms. Joanne's big orange belly was squashed between them but she didn't mind at all. There was a first time for everything and this evening was one of many firsts.

EPILOGUE

Autumn had passed and winter was settling over Wisteria Hollow bringing cold dark mornings and biting winds that made Joanne's teeth chatter as she walked to and from work and to the library, which she did more often now. Things were going well with Max and they'd been out on more dates, but they were taking their time getting to know each other and Joanne was enjoying it immensely.

Her financial situation was the healthiest it had been for a long time. Using the money from her parents she had paid off all her debts and put the rest into a high interest savings account along with the proceeds from her eBay sales. She was keeping an eye on the property market but had yet to find the perfect house to buy. She had worried about being a burden on her parents but they'd insisted that they loved having her there. When her mum had hugged her tight and told her that she wanted her there for a big family Christmas, Joanne had felt reassured that she could take her time and find the right house for her.

As for Kerry and Jeremy, they seemed to be more in love and committed than ever. Kerry had applied for the job and been invited for interview, but when she'd gone to the school she'd realised that it wasn't quite right for her. She was still looking though, and had Jeremy's full support; he'd said that he would happily work freelance if it came down to moving. Kerry had also spoken to Jeremy about how they'd made Joanne feel, and when they'd come for Sunday lunch a few weeks ago, the three of them had sat down together and he had apologised for being an idiot. They were all coming for Christmas and Joanne was looking forward to it, knowing that the tensions that had previously existed had been dispersed and she could relax with her family and be herself at last.

Joanne grabbed her bag and skipped down the stairs then put her coat on and pulled a woolly hat over her hair. She was off to Lila's for lunch and Roxie was coming too. Apparently Lila had some news for them but she'd refused to say a word about it until they were together and Joanne's curiosity was piqued.

Life was far more settled for her and her friends and it had been a good autumn on Sunflower Street. She was looking forward to seeing what winter would bring…

THE END

DEAR READER

Thank you so much for reading *Autumn Spice on Sunflower Street*. I hope you enjoyed the story.

If you can spare five minutes of your time, I would be so grateful if you could leave a rating and a short review.

You can find me on Twitter **@authorRG,** on Facebook at **Rachel Griffiths Author** and on Instagram at **rachelgriffithsauthor** if you'd like to connect with me to find out more about my books and what I'll be working on next.

With love,
Rachel X

ABOUT THE AUTHOR

Rachel Griffiths is an author, wife, mother, Earl Grey tea drinker, gin enthusiast, dog walker and fan of the afternoon nap. She loves to read, write and spend time with her family.

ALSO BY RACHEL GRIFFITHS

CWTCH COVE SERIES

CHRISTMAS AT CWTCH COVE

WINTER WISHES AT CWTCH COVE

MISTLETOE KISSES AT CWTCH COVE

THE COTTAGE AT CWTCH COVE

THE CAFÉ AT CWTCH COVE

CAKE AND CONFETTI AT CWTCH COVE

A NEW ARRIVAL AT CWTCH COVE

THE COSY COTTAGE CAFÉ SERIES

SUMMER AT THE COSY COTTAGE CAFÉ

AUTUMN AT THE COSY COTTAGE CAFÉ

WINTER AT THE COSY COTTAGE CAFÉ

SPRING AT THE COSY COTTAGE CAFÉ

A WEDDING AT THE COSY COTTAGE CAFÉ

A YEAR AT THE COSY COTTAGE CAFÉ (THE COMPLETE SERIES)

THE LITTLE CORNISH GIFT SHOP SERIES

CHRISTMAS AT THE LITTLE CORNISH GIFT SHOP

SPRING AT THE LITTLE CORNISH GIFT SHOP

SUMMER AT THE LITTLE CORNISH GIFT SHOP

THE LITTLE CORNISH GIFT SHOP (THE COMPLETE SERIES)

SUNFLOWER STREET SERIES

SPRING SHOOTS ON SUNFLOWER STREET

SUMMER DAYS ON SUNFLOWER STREET

AUTUMN SPICE ON SUNFLOWER STREET

CHRISTMAS WISHES ON SUNFLOWER STREET

A WEDDING ON SUNFLOWER STREET

A NEW BABY ON SUNFLOWER STREET

NEW BEGINNINGS ON SUNFLOWER STREET

SNOWFLAKES AND CHRISTMAS CAKES ON SUNFLOWER STREET

A YEAR ON SUNFLOWER STREET (SUNFLOWER STREET BOOKS 1-4)

THE COSY COTTAGE ON SUNFLOWER STREET

SNOWED IN ON SUNFLOWER STREET

SPRINGTIME SURPRISES ON SUNFLOWER STREET

AUTUMN DREAMS ON SUNFLOWER STREET

A CHRISTMAS TO REMEMBER ON SUNFLOWER STREET

STANDALONE STORIES

CHRISTMAS AT THE LITTLE COTTAGE BY THE SEA

THE WEDDING

ACKNOWLEDGMENTS

Thanks go to:

My gorgeous family. I love you so much! XXX

My author and blogger friends, for your support, advice and encouragement.

Everyone who buys, reads and reviews this book.

Printed in Great Britain
by Amazon